ISBN: 9798388385123

Imprint: Independently published

FROSTFALL ISLAND
COZY MYSTERY SERIES

LONDON LOVETT

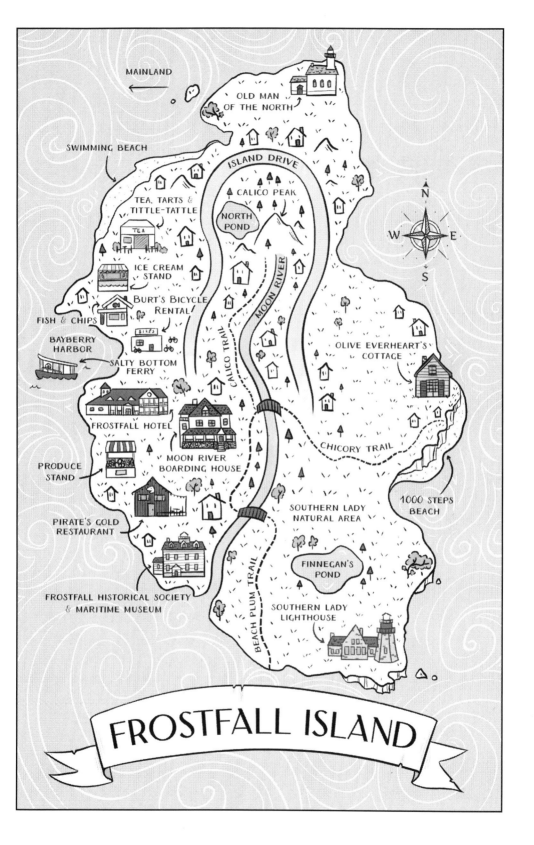

FROSTFALL ISLAND

one

THE SKY WAS a mix of coral and peach as the great glowing orb lifted its head above the horizon. I was alone, the last woman on earth, watching as the new dawn sun grew from the sea. It would be up to me and me alone to restart humanity. I had so many ideas, so many plans to make it different from the first try. Kindness would prevail. Suffering would be banished. Reading would be required, and there would be a law against wearing those weird plastic Croc shoes. Granted, the last one was on a more personal level, but if I was to lead the world back from the brink, I would insist upon it. Huck's cold nose pushed against the back of my hand, and my big, mostly altruistic daydream vanished.

I patted Huck's soft head. His thick fur was wet from the spray of salty water along the shore where he'd spent the last fifteen minutes trying to snuffle horseshoe crabs out of the wet sand. His long legs were coated so thickly in sand it looked like he was wearing gray boots. Huck had chosen this morning's adventure. Once across the Moon River, he trotted with full determination toward Chicory Trail and Thousand Steps Beach. My original plan was to hike down to Finnegan's Pond and wait to see if the newly arrived red-winged blackbirds would cooperate for a quick watercolor. Every spring they returned to their favorite towering reeds at the end of the pond. Their throaty trilling sounds were quite possibly my favorite part of a new spring.

Two plovers landed near the water with their neat little black and white neck scarves and white tummies. Huck stared at them, apparently debating whether the two birds were worth another gallop down to the water. But his breakfast would be waiting at home, and a hungry, wingless dog was no match for the plovers. He barked once to let them know he was giving them the day off and then raced ahead toward the impossibly long flight of splintery wooden steps that would take us back to the trail. His sandy boots slowly fell away with each exuberant stride.

I stopped at the bottom of the steps and stared up at them as if I was staring up at Everest's peak. My tray of paints and paper pad, both untouched this morning, were tucked under my arm, ready for the journey skyward. "Small step for mankind," I muttered as my semi-wet shoe landed on step number one. First, I was restarting a new world, and now, I was an astronaut taking a step on a new planet. I wasn't sure where all the delusions of grandeur were coming from this morning. It might just have been the frenetic energy that came with a new spring. I loved Frostfall Island and rarely found fault with any of it, but winter was long and harsh and, for lack of a better word, suffocating. It seemed that every time the layer of snow had flattened to insignificance, a new, fresh blanket would fall. The whole island was layered with ice and powdery dust the entire season. I loved a snowy landscape, but after a few months, it felt as if nature, trees and all, had been erased. Even now, with spring already in firm control, small clumps of stubborn snow still clung to the succulent leaves of the sea sandwort that dotted the cliffs.

I'd always found it easiest to climb the endless flight of rickety steps by occupying my mind with other things, mostly edible things. Something about strenuous exercise always triggered thoughts of food. This morning there was a tray full of thick slices of fluffy brioche waiting to be dipped and battered and griddled into French toast. A bowl of strawberries waited to be sliced for topping, and, of course, whipped butter and powdered sugar would be added to the list. I normally saved French toast for the weekend and never for a Monday, but the beauty of spring had inspired me, and strawberry topped French toast drowning in maple syrup and butter seemed like a perfect way to start the week.

I reached the top of the steps and had a sudden urge to pump my fists and dance around triumphantly like Sylvester Stallone in *Rocky*. There were no lights on at Olive's house. My dear friend and most sought after confidant liked to sleep late. She preferred the hours before and after midnight for her artistic endeavors. She'd created a unique niche for herself with paint by number artwork. Olive had also learned to tune out the criticism that poked at her from every corner of the internet. She'd found her calling, and she had enough fans and art customers to keep herself financially sound. It helped that her rock and roll singing parrot, Johnny, was an internet sensation. *My* best buddy's talent, on the other hand, was scaring squirrels and leaving muddy footprints in the kitchen. This morning there would be more sand than mud.

Huck trotted ahead. The dog was equally pleased to be out from the heavy mantle of a long, dreary winter. Spring meant new critters to harass and fresh smells to follow. He paused for a second and wiggled his nose in the direction of the pond and Beach Plum Trail, our usual path. Huck and I had made it a tradition to stop at the curve on Beach Plum Trail and stare out at the rippling ocean. It was the last place we both stood to watch Michael's boat, *Wild Rose,* motor out to sea. We continued the tradition long after Michael's disappearance. It had to be much harder, more confusing for an animal. All Huck knew was Michael sailed off that day, and he still hadn't returned. He didn't realize that his friend was never coming back. Lately, it seemed, I looked that direction less and less. The hurt, the agony of losing Michael lessened with time. And... if I was being brutally honest with myself, something I wasn't apt to do... my broken heart had been distracted by a new person in my life.

Nate was just leaving the house as Huck and I crossed over the river. His smile could melt away every layer of a winter's frost. Nathaniel had arrived at Frostfall Island a sullen, moody man who'd been broken by the ills of society. He gave up his job as a city detective, hoping to hide away from civilization and find solace on a mostly deserted island.

I was sure, just like me, he hadn't expected to find someone to help him discover happiness again. I certainly didn't expect it when I first met the man. But that was what had happened, and slowly, we'd both become each other's favorite companion. We'd helped each other see that somewhere in darkness there was always light.

"I expected to see you two coming from the other direction." Nate was wearing his heavy work boots and a blue flannel shirt that looked breathtakingly good on him. (I knew it was breathtaking because I literally had to catch my breath.) The new spring sun had deepened his skin to a glowing bronze, which made his smile even whiter. Along with retrieving the breath that had been swept out of me, I had to fortify my knees that tended to get a little wobbly at first sight of him.

"I'd planned to go down to the pond, but Huck had other ideas." We stopped just inches from each other.

Nate lifted his metal lunch pail. He'd given up law enforcement, where death and disappointment had nearly destroyed him for good, and he'd found a new purpose in construction. He claimed working with his hands was the therapy he needed. I liked to think Frostfall, his housemates and his *landlord* had helped too. "Thanks for the sandwiches. The rest of the crew always hovers around waiting with envy to see what I have in my lunch. If I'd had lunches like this in grammar school, I could have made a fortune with a side hustle of selling my lunch. They might have even let me sit at the popular table."

I laughed. "Something tells me you were already at that

table, delicious lunch or not. In fact, I'll bet you were at the head of that table."

Nate grinned shyly. "All I know is I somehow managed to land the prom queen on this island."

"Sorry, that was my sister, Cora. Prom queen, homecoming queen, most likely to be a movie star, you name it she won it."

Nate took hold of my hand and pulled me gently into his arms for a kiss. He lifted his mouth from mine and gazed at me with those dark blue eyes. "And yet, she's got nothing on you."

I kissed him lightly before he released me. "Boy oh boy, where were you when fourteen-year-old Anna, the troll living under her sister's glow-casting shadow, needed you?"

"Hmm, I was sitting at the head of the popular kid's table."

I nudged his stomach with my fist. "See, I knew it."

"Actually, I spent far more time in the principal's office than at the lunch tables, but that's a story for another day. I've got to get to the lighthouse. We're starting earlier, like the sun."

"I wish I'd known that. I'm making French toast this morning."

"I saw all the trimmings. Even considered calling the boss to let him know I'd be late, but the workers who show up late have to carry the lumber and tools off the truck." Nate had gotten lucky. Jobs were not plentiful on the island, especially once the summer crowds had vanished, but Frostfall had received big grants from the Maritime Historical Society to restore the island's two lighthouses. The Old Man of the North stood guard watching over the ships and sailors on the northern tip of the island, and the Southern Lady stood regally, like an elegant matron, on the southern end. The construction crew needed workers, and Nate had found a job rather quickly. As much as I would've liked to credit myself for him sticking around long past his initial six month lease, I knew the job gave him a reason to stay. He loved working on the old lighthouses. "Beats chasing down serial killers," he'd said to me more than once after a long day on the site.

"I'll save you some French toast for a midnight snack."

"And that is why I'm totally bonkers for my landlady. Later, Huck." My dog had tried more than once to follow his favorite person to work, but he'd finally learned that if Nate was carrying the silver lunch pail, he was stuck with boring old me.

I waited for Nate to reach the bridge. He waved and I blew him a kiss. My heart did a little skip and jump as his boots thumped on the wooden bridge. I held my breath for a moment, savoring the happiness, but as I released it, those irritating, cynical thoughts that occasionally cluttered my reasoning surfaced again. I'd been happy before, and it ended in terrible heartbreak.

"Argh, Mom, I'm blaming you for my bouts of pessimism," I muttered. My mom always liked to remind Cora and me that happiness was fleeting. This time she was wrong. This time my happily ever after was going to last. Hopefully.

two

OPAL WAS the first person at the table. Rather than standing up in quirky spikes, her fiery red hair drooped down like melted wax. Dark circles were becoming a permanent fixture on her face. "Another bad night?" I asked as I put my painting supplies on my desk.

"Is it that obvious? I don't know what's wrong with me. One minute I'm sitting in front of the television, so drowsy I can't keep my eyes open, even with Cary Grant on the screen, and the next, I'm in bed, blanket to my chin, pillow fluffed to perfection under my head and I'm staring at the ceiling counting movie stars." Years ago, Opal's past life came to her in a dream. It turned out, according to my dear friend, that she was the devilishly handsome, impossible to resist Rudolph Valentino in a previous life. Ever since that day, Opal had dedicated most of her retired life to watching old movie classics. Some people counted sheep, but Opal counted movie stars. Lately, the parade of long since passed celebrities had not been helping her sleep. She'd been struggling with insomnia for several weeks, and it was really starting to take a toll on her.

"I've got a plan," I said. I ran a boarding house, but the people renting my rooms were far more than tenants. They were family, my own quirky, wonderful family. That included my sister, Cora, who was more eccentric than quirky, but I was still thrilled to have her back in my life. I sat down across from Opal. She looked about as weary as I'd ever seen her. Even the soft wrinkles around her eyes and mouth were hanging down as if gravity was pulling on them. "First of all, I'm going to make you decaf." Her reaction time had slowed from lack of sleep. She reached for her cup of coffee a few seconds after I'd snatched it out from under her.

"Decaf?" she asked with a sour twist of her mouth. "Isn't that like eating sugar-free brownies or low-fat croissants? Inferior products that pretend to be as good as the real thing but fall sadly short?"

"You won't know the difference. After Michael vanished, I spent hours lying in bed waiting for sleep to come. I switched to decaffeinated coffee and it helped."

Opal lifted a tired brow. "But you switched back to caffeinated?"

"Well, yes, but that's only because I no longer have any trouble sleeping. Now, are you interested in hearing the rest of my plan or not?"

Even her sigh sounded exhausted. "Anything if it'll help me get some good sleep."

"You're going to cut way down on the movie marathons and start walking with me. You need exercise."

Opal stared up at me from under the red bangs that were hanging like limp curtains on her forehead. "Maybe I can just get used to not sleeping."

"Come on, Opal. It'll be fun. You can walk with me to Sera's tea shop this morning. Then we can stop at the produce stand."

"What about Sera's tea shop?" Cora asked as she entered the kitchen. "Oh, by the way, I passed Winston on the way to the bathroom. He told me to let you know he was heading out early. Alyssa"—she said with a smile—"loves the chocolate croissants at the new bakery." For well over a year, our youngest housemate, Winston, had been hiding the crush he had on his boss, Alyssa. She ran the Frostfall Wildlife Rescue on the north shore. Winston finally let her know his feelings. It turned out she felt the same. We were all excited for him. That was life on an island. Small bursts of things turning out just right were always cause for celebration.

"Darn, I have all this French toast." I stared at the stack of brioche slices.

"More for us," Opal said. "I'm going to need the fuel since you're making me walk the island like some kind of gladiator."

Cora laughed as she poured herself a cup of coffee. "Where are you two trekking to? The Coliseum?"

"Just to the 3Ts." I pulled the egg and milk mixture out of the refrigerator. "I thought a good, long walk might help alleviate Opal's insomnia."

10

"Are you still having trouble sleeping?" Cora shook her smooth blonde curls. "Thank goodness I've never had insomnia. My head hits the pillow, and I'm out like Sleeping Beauty." Most people used the out like a light analogy, but not my sister. She would much prefer to compare herself to a Disney princess than something as mundane as a light bulb.

"That, dear sister, is because you never fret or worry or overthink anything. You fall asleep knowing full well that you'll wake up the next morning as stunning Cora and that somewhere in the world your Prince Charming is waiting to kiss you, take care of you and buy you expensive diamond watches." As I said it, she twisted her sparkling watch on her slim wrist.

"It would be nice to have some new diamonds. And a new Prince Charming, for that matter." Cora sat with her coffee. "By the way, it's good you're going to visit Seraphina this morning. She's extremely distraught about this new French bakery on the island."

Just as winter came to its chilly close, Quentin Oxley, a French trained pastry chef and master baker arrived to open up his Parisian Bakery. I'd yet to make a trip to the new shop, but he'd already gained a loyal following.

I lifted the bread slices from their eggy bath and dropped them onto the buttered griddle. I had to speak loudly over the sizzle. "Sera's got nothing to worry about," I said. "People love her tarts, and her incredible selection of exotic teas brings tourists to the island. People will tire of chocolate croissants and French pastries. It's just the novelty of having a new shop on the island."

"That's what you should say to Sera. Although, I'm not sure it'll help much. Yesterday, I waited on three people," Cora said.

"At a time?" Opal asked.

"Nope, for my entire shift."

I dropped my spatula and spun around. "Three customers for the entire morning?" I asked. "You're exaggerating."

Cora straightened the neckline on her low-cut dress. "Wish I were. I made exactly seven dollars in tips. Do you know what you can buy with seven dollars these days? Nothing. That's what. Actually, you can get one of those chocolate croissants with a few pennies leftover."

"See, that's expensive. People, especially locals, will run out of pocket money for those overpriced baked goods. Sera just has to weather this lull." I was feeling a little neglectful of my good friend, Seraphina Butterpond, and her wonderful husband, Samuel. She'd seemed distracted and a little down, not in character for Sera, the last few times I stopped in for tea. While I'd noticed the shop was quieter than usual, I'd brushed it off as a late start to the spring. I hadn't considered that the new bakery would be a competitor for her business. Tea, Tarts and Tittle-tattle, or the 3Ts as we called it, was by far the most popular stop for tourists and locals. Her business was always booming so much she often complained that she had way too much work to do.

The door opened and Tobias stepped inside. "The weather was perfect for a swim, but the bay was a little choppy." Tobias, or Toby as we called him, kept himself fit as a teenager with a long swim at the beach every morning. He was truly the gladiator. There could be frost on the sand and the waves could be tipped with snow and ice but he still swam. He lifted his nose. "I smell French toast."

"Yes, and I will leave yours plain and place some strawberries in a bowl. They're super sweet right now." Tobias was a warrior when it came to swimming in freezing temperatures, but when it came to his plate, he was a fussy toddler. No foods could touch each other, and everything had to be eaten separately. He even skipped butter and maple syrup on his French toast because the egg and milk coating was already pushing it.

Tobias patted his stomach. "Just two pieces of toast this morning, Anna." Tobias shrugged coyly. When he first moved into the house, he was shy and awkward in conversations. He was an accountant. He'd told me more than once if numbers had been people, he'd have been the most popular man in town because he got along much better with numbers. But he was much more comfortable now. He'd occasionally withdraw into his awkward shell if Cora was at the table, but even the impact of her presence had worn off.

"Tobias?" I asked. "Is something up?"

He sighed and pulled the beach towel off his shoulder. "All right, the guilt is getting to me. Anna, I've been stopping at the new bakery on my way to work. He bakes the flakiest, most buttery croissants I have ever tasted."

I laughed. "You don't have to feel guilty about that, Toby. I'm a little jealous but then I can't make a decent croissant to save my life. Just can't get the technique down." My competitive side was already nudging me to spend the afternoon on YouTube learning how to make croissants.

Tobias was so relieved his whole posture melted. "I'm so glad to have that off my shoulders." His sensitive nose wriggled. "Along with this wet towel. I'm going to put it in the laundry room. It needs a wash. I'll be right down for breakfast after a quick shower."

I dropped two slices of toast into the egg wash. The four pieces on the griddle were cooked to perfection. I lifted them onto plates and put a dollop of whipped butter on each. As I spun around from the stove, Opal and Cora were watching me with interest.

"What's wrong?" I reached up to see if I had something on my face.

"Nothing's wrong," Cora said teasingly. She turned to Opal. "How much do you want to bet my sister spends the rest of the day learning to make croissants?" My sister knew me too well and vice versa. That was what happened when your parents were divorced and you had to count on your sibling more than your parent. Cora was older and she was incredibly beautiful and popular, but she always looked after me. She never treated me like an annoying little sister, and I was pleased that I could repay her for that by offering her a home.

"I won't take that bet," Opal said, "because I know it's true."

I lifted my chin in defiance. "Nope, not true. I've got too much to do today, like taking my friend Opal out for a nice, bracing walk."

Opal slumped but it wasn't from exhaustion. "I was hoping Tobias' alarming confession would have doused your enthusiasm for a walk."

"If anything, it has invigorated me. So eat up and then put on your dancing shoes, my dear, because we're going to hit the trails."

three

PREFERRING silky chiffon house dresses with flowing sleeves and hems, Opal didn't have much in the way of outdoor gear, but she managed to cobble together an outfit suitable for a walk with a pair of gray slacks and a button up paisley print shirt. I lent her a straw hat, and she put on her most practical shoes, which were closer to being slippers than actual shoes.

We'd taken a nice jaunt along Beach Plum Trail before heading toward the harbor and town. After a few minutes of grumbling about her shoes not being ideal for the uneven trail, she found her rhythm and even seemed to be enjoying herself.

"I must say, you look better already. Your cheeks are rosy, and those dark circles have faded," I noted. I'd had to slow my normal pace considerably, but it was worth it to see Opal looking more energetic than I'd seen in a long time.

"I feel better. I think when I get back to the house, I'll take a long nap."

"No," I said a little too sharply. "I mean go ahead if you feel you need it, but a long nap will mess up your nighttime sleep. You need to get yourself back in a normal sleep pattern. Maybe you should take up a hobby, like knitting or jigsaw puzzles. Something to keep you more occupied during the day so that you'll sleep at night."

"I suppose you're right, but I don't really see myself as a knitter, or a puzzler, for that matter. I do like to read. Maybe I'll hop online and order myself some books. I love those scary Stephen King novels."

"Those might not be great for your insomnia either." I laughed. We were heading back toward town, and I, instinctually, stopped to stare out at the place where I last saw Michael. Opal caught my pensive moment.

"You still think about him a lot, don't you?" she asked quietly.

I pulled my gaze away. "I think that's mostly because there was never true closure. It's one thing to have someone die and have that death confirmed. I know it sounds crazy, but sometimes, I get the sense that he's still alive, that he's living somewhere, maybe on an exotic island."

"Like a castaway?" Opal asked. "Wouldn't that be a story? There's a wonderful movie with Doris Day and James Garner where she was stranded on an island with a very dreamy Chuck Connors and then she's rescued..." Her words trailed off. "I guess that's not the best movie to talk about at this time. I'm blaming it on my lack of sleep."

17

I put my arm around her shoulder and squeezed her. "I've seen that movie and it is wonderful. And, if Michael did get stranded on a deserted island with a beautiful woman that would be far better than the alternative. Now, enough about that. Do you have enough energy to walk to town? I still need to visit Sera's shop."

"I can go a bit further, but at the risk of sounding like a traitor, I'll part ways with you on the boardwalk."

I looked questioningly at her. "You're planning on visiting the bakery."

"Just want to see what the all fuss is about. But I solemnly swear that I will not enjoy any of the baked goods more than yours."

"All right, I guess if you're going to solemnly swear." We walked back toward the harbor. It became instantly apparent that a flow of people were heading toward the new bakery. My good friend Jack Drake's pirate themed restaurant was right next door to the bakery, but it was too early for the lunch crowd, and while his place did well, I'd never noticed an actual movement of people in that direction.

"I guess there's going to be a line." Opal stopped.

"It seems there will be a long line. Do you want me to walk you back to the house?" I asked.

"No, no, go and see Sera. It's no wonder she's worried. I'll get in line, and if it's taking too long, I'll head back home on my own." She winked at me. "I promise I won't get lost."

"Right. Sorry. I just wanted to make sure you were all right on your own. After all, this has been a pretty long trek."

"It has and I'm feeling proud of myself. Proud enough to

reward myself with one of those fancy French pastries. I'll see you back at home." Opal strolled away. Her steps were amazingly peppy considering how far we'd walked this morning. I was feeling confident about my plan to ease her insomnia. As long as she didn't spend the rest of the day napping, she should be able to drop right off into movie star dreamland tonight.

A good portion of my morning had been used for Opal's walk. Sera would not be expecting me at this hour. I normally stopped by early, drank a cup of tea, then made my way back to the harbor for my produce and a dose of gossip.

I picked up my pace, knowing I still had plenty to do today but also wanting to make sure I didn't rush my visit with Sera. If she was feeling down, then I needed to be there for her. She'd been my main support person as I navigated my way through tragedy. Not that I would equate the two events. I was still sure the new bakery would lose its *sugary shine* soon, and Sera's customers would return. With that firm thought in my head, I nearly froze when I saw how stunningly empty the tea shop was. The weather was nice enough for tea at the outside tables but, aside from two sad looking pigeons, the chairs were empty. The inside tables were just as deserted.

Sera was standing at her counter, wiping it absently, as she stared out the window at her empty tables and chairs. "Well, I guess this is it for the 3Ts," Sera said grimly.

Samuel poked his head out to see who she was talking to. "Oh, Anna, it's you. Thought we had a customer."

I headed toward my favorite stool and sat down. "I am a

customer," I said confidently. "I'll take one of your savory egg and cheese tarts and a cup of oolong tea."

"Are you sure I can't interest you in a dozen egg tarts and a dozen strawberry ones?" Sera shuffled over to the teapots. Sera was not a shuffler. She usually walked with a prance like a circus pony. Things were bad.

"We're having movie night tomorrow evening. I could buy them and put them in my freezer. Maybe heat them in the oven prior to the movie."

Sera poured me some oolong. It had a spicy, malted scent. "I'm just kidding." She returned with the cup of tea.

I took extra long to savor the sip so she remembered just how good her tea tasted. "I'll bet even King Charles can't brew a cuppa like you."

She poured herself a cup. "Something tells me King Charles does not brew his own tea. In fact, I'll bet he's got a team of people just to make his tea. But you're right, it still wouldn't be as good as my tea. Oh, Anna, I just don't know what we'll do. Did you run into Cora on your way here? I sent her home. There's nothing for her to do."

"Opal and I were out on a walk, so I didn't see her." I glanced around at the empty room. Sera's whimsical decorations, the chains of silk roses and the fresh flowers on the tables all looked somber with no one to enjoy them. It was time for a pep talk. I'd been on the receiving end of Sera's many times. It was my turn to be the cheer squad. "Like I told Cora this morning, people will get tired of those fancy baked goods. He charges a lot of money for those goodies, and when people start realizing their pockets are empty and their bellies are bigger, they're going to end their bakery habit. People will come back to the place they know and love. They'll come back to the 3Ts. Now, I insist the two of you come to movie night tomorrow at seven. Opal has chosen the double feature. We start the evening with Bela Lugosi and end it on a much sweeter note—Doris Day. I'll see you then."

Sera didn't look too convinced, even though I gave her little leeway to reject the invite. "I'll see how we're feeling. We don't want to come and ruin the whole mood with our sourpusses."

Samuel had been working in the back, but the shop was so empty he could hear our entire conversation. He popped out from the back room. "Speak for yourself," he said. "I'm not sour. I agree with Anna. People will tire of those rich, expensive pastries. We just have to wait it out. Pretty soon, it'll be summer, and you'll be complaining that we have way too much business."

Sera smiled weakly. "And he's dreamy to look at too. You're right, Sam. We'll just have to be patient. I can use all the spare time to create some new tarts. I've been thinking about making some with candied orange peels and ginger."

"I want in on that taste test." I stood up from the stool. "I've got to get to Molly's stand before she runs out of strawberries. I used up all of mine on French toast at breakfast. And, if it makes you feel any better, my delicious French toast was pushed aside for croissants this morning. Winston left early just to get in line. But I forgive him because he's trying to impress his new girlfriend."

"Ah yes, new love." Sera reached for Samuel's hand and kissed it.

"We've been married for three years," Samuel reminded her.

"And it still feels like the first day we met."

I tapped the counter. "Maybe this break will be nice. You two should plan a picnic and some romantic nights." It was a silly suggestion because romance had never been a problem with the pair. "See you tomorrow night," I said as I walked out.

The morning had really gotten away from me. I needed to get to the produce stand.

four

MOLLY PICKERING, Frostfall's main purveyor of quality produce, was standing beneath the shade of one of her signature straw hats. It had a wide enough brim to keep her nose and round apple cheeks from getting sunburned. The brim tipped up. Her smile sparkled under the shade of the hat. "You're late, my friend." She reached behind her shelves of baskets and emerged with a container of plump red strawberries. "Get 'em while they're good."

I reached for the basket. "So it's true. It *is* good to have friends in high places. Thanks for putting some aside. They really are spring jewels."

Molly motioned toward the tea shop. "Were you visiting with Seraphina?"

"Yes." It was hard not to frown.

"I've heard. All of her customers have been spending their spare change at the new bakery. Quentin Oxley, a very arrogant man, by the way, has taken this island by storm. Or in his case, by yeast dough and sugary toppings. Have you met him?" she asked.

"I haven't even been by the bakery yet. I guess I'm reluctant to try his treats because then I'll realize how truly inferior my baked goods are."

"Nonsense. People are enamored with the whole French part of it. They think they're continental and worldly because they're eating pastries created by a French trained chef. They'll tire of it soon enough."

"Have you sampled any of his goodies?" I asked as I picked yellow potatoes for a potato salad.

"I've bought his sourdough bread a few times." She rolled in her lips as if not sure whether to continue.

"Well? Don't keep me in suspense." I dropped six potatoes into the shopping basket.

"It was the best sourdough bread I've ever tasted. Apparently, his sourdough starter is over a hundred years old and a family treasure."

"I don't know how people do that. I've restarted my *starter* so many times it's like a cat with nine lives."

Remi Seymour, a local in her mid thirties, rolled past on her bicycle. Her long black hair looked particularly shiny in the sunlight. Remi always wore shorts to show off her long, lovely legs. She rode her bicycle everywhere, which was probably the reason for her legs being so lovely. She lived on the island near the swim beach and worked remotely for a financial firm. She was dating Jamie Baxter, a Frostfall fisherman. Michael and Jamie occasionally went out on catches together. In a sense, Jamie learned his fishing skills from Michael.

24

Remi stopped at the bike racks across from the produce stand. Shorts and all, she was dressed fancy for a casual bike ride. She had on a shimmering pink camisole top and blue suede ankle boots. I waved as she climbed off the bike, but she didn't wave back. She seemed distracted. Remi wrapped the black cable of her bike lock around the bike and the metal rack. She snapped the lock closed and headed off.

"I'll bet she's going to the bakery," Molly said.

"Like everyone else."

"Only she might not just be going there for the croissants," Molly said with a lilt in her tone that hinted at some forthcoming gossip. I tried like the dickens to avoid getting caught up in too much island gossip, and with Frostfall being a small island, it was rampant and moved at the speed of light. The tittle-tattle end of Sera's shop was a literal invitation for locals to come in, eat tarts, sip tea and exchange interesting tidbits.

I scooted closer with my basket of potatoes. Molly had grabbed my full attention. "What do you mean? Is she going to the bakery for... *brownies*?" I added, in a suspenseful tone.

Molly laughed. "No, I mean Remi is supposedly sweet on something at that bakery, and it doesn't have to do with the goodies behind the glass." She tilted her head side to side. "Well, technically, he's behind the glass."

I straightened with surprise. The little potatoes rolled across the bottom of the basket and bounced off the side. "You mean Remi is seeing the new baker?"

"That's what Jen and Pauline told me when there were here buying onions and carrots for stew. They'd been at the

25

bakery one morning, early, so they could get one of the highly coveted chocolate croissants, and they saw Remi leaving the bakery." She said the last part as if it was a big ta-da ending, but it fell somewhat flat.

"So?" I asked.

"Oh, I guess I forgot the most important part. The bakery wasn't open yet."

"Ah, I see. I'm sorry to hear it if that's true. Jamie Baxter will be heartbroken."

"Morning, Molly, morning, Anna." Frannie Bueller's husband, Joe, had one of those salty, scratchy voices that you'd expect from a man who'd spent a great deal of time out on the ocean. He'd captained several merchant vessels before deciding to slow his life down and run the ferry service from Frostfall to the mainland with his wife.

I turned around to greet him. He had that leathery look of a lifelong sailor as well. The lines on his face were like an intricate map, and they got deeper and bolder with each passing year. But leathery old sea captain that he was, he still always charmed with his lopsided smile.

"Joe, I was just about to head over to the dock to say hi to Fran," I said. "I see by your captain's hat you're in charge today."

"Fran's got a sore throat." Joe picked an orange out of the citrus basket and started peeling it. "Put it on my tab," he told Molly.

"You don't actually have a tab because this is a produce stand and not a pub but enjoy, Joe. I know how you old pirates are when it comes to keeping away scurvy."

Joe's barrel laugh fit perfectly with the rest of him. He was a big man, over six feet tall, and his shoulders were so big Frannie had to order shirts online for him because the stores never had the right size. He set about, with massive, calloused tipped fingers, peeling the orange. It was a full sized navel orange, but it looked like a tiny mandarin in his hand. The summery fragrance of the orange filled the air.

"I'm sorry to hear that Fran isn't feeling well," I said. "Maybe you should take her a few of those oranges."

"Good idea. I've also been asked—no—*commanded* to stop by the new bakery for some cheese Danish."

I looked at Molly. "Everyone's got French bakery fever."

"Yep and I don't think that fever's going away anytime soon," Molly said.

I glanced down the boardwalk. The bright blue awning over Sera's outdoor tables rippled in the wind. "Poor Sera," I muttered. I paid for my produce and decided maybe it was time for me to walk to the bakery and check it out. Was it really as good as everyone said?

five

THE WORDS PARISIAN Bakery were delicately painted across a large white sign. Blue and pink striped awnings covered the two front windows, and behind them, glass trays and triple tiered cake stands were filled with richly frosted cupcakes and pastries that resembled works of art. The building used to be a souvenir shop filled with t-shirts, postcards and tiny replicas of the Frostfall lighthouses. There were always two bins of assorted flavors of saltwater taffy sitting on each side of the door. Small model pirate ships, pirate hats and pirate's gold (chocolate coins) lined one wall to go along with the mostly fabricated pirate history of Frostfall Island. Carl and Connie, the owners, had decided to sell the place and move to the city. Carl was struggling with health issues, and Connie didn't want to run the store alone. The building sat vacant through the entire fall and winter. Then, one day, the realtor sign was gone, and slowly but surely, things were happening inside the shop. Most of us didn't know it was going to be a bakery until the sign went up. I remembered thinking it was going to be one of those mom and pop bakeries with cookies that all tasted the same, brownies topped with an oil based frosting, cakes covered in brightly colored icing and a small counter where you could get a cone of store-bought ice cream. Never would I have expected a trained pastry chef to bring his culinary skills to our small island. For now, it seemed to have been a good business choice, but I wondered for how long. I was sure the frenzy and excitement would die off. Eventually, with the prices Mr. Oxley had to charge to cover his overhead, people would realize the bakery didn't fit their budget.

The bakery sat right next to the Pirate's Gold Restaurant. It had been a perfect location for the souvenir shop. Tourists could come to this side of the boardwalk and get the entire buccaneer treatment with a lunch at the pirate themed restaurant, a trip to the souvenir store for a felt pirate's tricorn and a tour through the pirate filled museum just a half block down.

Jack Drake, the owner of the restaurant, was struggling, oddly enough, with a large, industrial-sized fan as he tried to set it up on the walkway outside the restaurant. Today's menu offered crab cakes and pirate's gold nuggets. A pungent seafood smell wafted out the open front door.

"Jack, why are you putting a fan out here?"

Jack's gray gaze lifted. Normally, he had a big smile for me, but today, something had soured his mood. "Anna, didn't see you there." Something was definitely off. At one point in time, it seemed that Jack Drake and I might have become more than just friends. Opal and Cora were certainly pushing for it, but my enthusiasm for the idea just never took hold. In the meantime, Jack had found someone, a woman who lived and worked on the mainland. He seemed genuinely happy. That was until right at this moment.

"Is something wrong, Jack?"

He glanced sharply at the bakery before turning back to me. "It's that baker. He keeps complaining that the aromas from my restaurant are ruining his baked goods and the whole *Parisian experience*." He said the last part with a heavy, snooty tone and a lift of his chin. It wasn't at all like Jack to be so angry. "He's threatening to go to the city council if I don't do something about it."

"Oh, Jack, that's terrible. Does he realize we don't actually have a city council?"

"I mentioned that to him, and he muttered something about knowing a lot of people with clout. He's the most arrogant person I've ever met." Jack squinted at me. "I suppose you were on your way to sample his goods. I think he uses way too much sugar and butter." He nodded. "Yes, that sounded even more ridiculous once it came out of my mouth."

I patted his arm. Unfortunately, I didn't have many suggestions to offer. The aromas from his restaurant usually lingered on the boardwalk all afternoon. It was good free advertisement. I was used to it and hardly noticed unless he was cooking something especially strong. I could see how those same aromas might not mesh well with baked goods.

No one wanted to smell fried crab cakes when they were biting into a strawberry Danish.

"So, you've resorted to trying to change the wind patterns with a big fan," I noted.

"It's either that or I stop cooking seafood and fried food and replace my entire menu with salads."

"I doubt Blackbeard was eating a strawberry spinach salad on deck." I was trying to make him smile, but it wasn't working. His dark brows were furrowed fast and steady over his eyes.

"Maybe you could help me," he said. "I'm going to turn this fan on. Go down the boardwalk toward the bakery and see if it helps."

"Aye, aye Cap'n." I saluted for good measure.

Behind me, the fan roared and made loud stuttering sounds as it pushed against the breeze flowing through its blades. It wasn't exactly ideal to have a large, noisy fan outside a restaurant. I walked past the few bakery customers still trying to get their chance inside the crowded shop. I stood just beyond the building and took several deep whiffs of air. An odd mix of smells wafted toward my nose. I could best describe it as cinnamon sugar toast that had been dipped in seafood sauce. And, on the outer edges of it all were the usual smells that were unique to living on an active harbor—engine diesel, the briny tang of the sea and the fishy odor that shrouded every boat tucked in the marina. I hated to break the news to Jack that his fan plan was not going to work.

I walked back to him. We had to move away from the

noise of the fan so we could hear each other over the industrial strength motor and the general clatter that four blades spinning at top speed could produce.

"Does it help?" Jack asked. He looked so distraught about it all, I badly wanted to say yes.

"I could still smell your crab cakes. That said, I don't have a comparison because I've never stood downwind from your restaurant and taken an intentional whiff of the air. Maybe with the fan it's better than it was."

Jack looked crestfallen. "I don't know what to do," he said. "I get the feeling this guy, Oxley, is prepared to make my life miserable just to get me to shut down."

"Do you think it'll get that drastic? This hasn't slowed down his business. There's been a line out here all morning."

"Trust me, I know. I tried to roll a dolly stacked with cans of tomatoes into my restaurant. No one would budge. Everyone was worried they'd lose their spot in line." He shook his head in dismay. "I had to wheel the dolly all the way down to the end of the line and back up to the restaurant. At first, I was excited that someone had finally bought that shop. Having it empty was not good for business, like in a shopping center when one of the shops just sits there boarded up and gathering dust. It brings down the whole center. I was equally glad to hear it would be a bakery. I've been known to chow down on a pastry or two for breakfast. Thought it would be a nice treat to have it right next door. Never did I consider that the aromas from my restaurant would become a problem."

"What about fans on the roof, near the kitchen vents," I offered but I knew very little about the subject.

"The wind would just kick it back anyhow." He walked over and turned off the fan. I realized then just how loud it was by the immediate silence.

"I don't think that fan will be a great draw for your customers either, Jack. It's loud and it'll be blowing people right through the door."

"Never thought of that. Oh well, I've taken up enough of your time with my problems," Jack said. "Everything good at home?"

"Yes, everything is good. And don't worry, Jack. Everything will work itself out." I said it with confidence, but I wasn't so sure. It was alarming how one person's arrival to the island could kick up so much happiness and trouble all at once.

six

I FELT RATHER traitorous as I stepped into the bakery line. Remi was leaned against the boardwalk railing, her long legs crossed at the ankles as she nibbled a chocolate chip cookie. I had to say, once I reached the inner sanctum of the Parisian Bakery, I could no longer smell Jack's crab cakes. The bakery was filled with that wondrous fragrance only a magical mix of yeast, butter and sugar could create. The interior décor was simple, with a lot of sparkling white marble, a few pieces of framed art and shiny chrome light pendants hanging over the glass front cases. Silver platters and cake stands stood behind the clear glass showing off artistic pastries of every shape and size along with some traditional favorites like fudge topped brownies and sugar dusted lemon bars. I considered my brownies to be my greatest achievement with a whisk and mixing bowl, so I decided to buy a brownie and do some comparisons. I worried that I'd be brought down to a brutal reality about my own brownies once I tasted Mr. Oxley's.

A small folded placard on top of the glass cases read 'out of croissants and Danish for the day'. There were three people in front of me. All were trying to decide what to choose. Sally Hogan was standing behind the counter looking harried and a little exhausted from the morning's rush. Sally and her husband, Murray, had lived on the island for twenty years. She used to work for Carl and Connie back when the shop was filled with souvenirs and stale saltwater taffy. Sally spotted me and waved weakly. One person behind the counter was not going to cut it if the shop continued to be this busy. Quentin Oxley's photo and a framed certificate showcasing his culinary training in Paris was on the wall next to the bins of breads. Most of the bread was also sold out for the day. There was one loaf of sourdough looking lonely and neglected. I decided to buy it for lunch.

The swinging door to the kitchen popped open, and the man himself strolled out. His chef's coat and hat were pristine and white. He cast a polite smile my direction. I supposed, to some people Quentin would be considered handsome, but he was far too polished for my taste. His symmetrical, sharp features almost made him look harsh, like an elegant villain. His smile faded as he reached Sally. I thought he'd come out to help behind the counter, but it turned out he'd emerged to lecture her.

"You're handling those cookies as if you have lobster claws for hands," he snapped. "How many times do I have to tell you—gently. Everything behind this glass is a masterpiece, and you must treat them that way. I will deduct all the broken pieces from your paycheck if you don't show more care."

Sally's face grew to a tomato shade of red. He was berating her like a child, and with the most condescending tone I'd ever heard. Fortunately, something outside caught his eye, a pair of long, tanned legs, I surmised. He put an end to his scolding, circled around the counter and walked out the door.

By the time I reached the front of the line, Sally was shaking with embarrassment.

"Sally, it's all right," I said. "He's probably just getting used to managing his bakery, and he probably didn't expect so much business right off the bat."

Sally forced a smile. "He's disappointed there's not a longer line. And he's managed other bakeries, so that's not an excuse either." She paused and took a deep breath. "I just have to not be so sensitive. But it's been nonstop all morning. I haven't even gotten a coffee break. What can I get you, Anna?"

"I'll take a brownie and that last loaf of sourdough."

Just like with Sera and Jack, there wasn't much I could say to help the situation. I paid for my baked goods and thanked Sally, telling her to hang in there. It was bound to get easier. I walked out thinking they were hollow words. Seeing Quentin in action, I doubted he would get any easier to work for. He might have been talented with dough and batters, but he lacked a few people skills.

I'd been right about the object of Quentin's focus after his unnecessary tongue lashing of his singular overworked sales-person. Quentin had leaned against the same railing as Remi. Their shoulders were touching. He lightly stroked her arm as he spoke to her. There was no way to misinterpret the scene. They were flirting, and by all indications, there was a lot more going on than a baker asking whether or not his customer enjoyed her cookie.

I tried to hide the bread and brownie as I hurried past Jack's restaurant. I took a bite of the brownie once I was clear of his windows. It was good but not nearly as good as mine. I laughed out loud in relief. My phone buzzed with a text jostling me out of my mirth. It was a text from Nate.

"Hey, I've got a friend coming out to the island for a few days. I'll give him the bed and sleep on the floor. I can pay extra for food and accommodations. Is that all right?"

I texted back. "Absolutely, your friend can stay. There are two spare guest rooms. He can use one of those, so you don't have to sleep on the floor."

"Best landlady ever," he texted back.

"I feel like a gray hunched old woman when you call me landlady."

He sent back two red hearts. I was sure he was busy, so I didn't respond. Not that there was any particular response to two hearts. That was the nice thing about emojis. They were good endpoints for a text conversation, sort of a last word without there actually being a word.

I stuck the phone in my pocket and folded the rest of the brownie up in its tissue wrapper. No need to waste the calo-ries, I thought with a satisfied smirk. Although, I had to admit the sourdough did smell wonderful. I was going to need to get home and figure out dinner. We rarely had guests. Which brought me to the question—just who was this mystery visitor? Nate rarely talked about any people he knew on the mainland. His best friend now was Sera's husband, Samuel. A love of mountain biking had brought the two men together and I was thrilled. The more friends and people Nate had on the island, the more likely he'd make this place his permanent home. I'd let my guard slip when it came to Nathaniel Maddon, and as much as I hated to admit it, I'd be devastated if he packed up and left the island. Hopefully, the visitor didn't have plans to talk Nate back into the civilization he'd so keenly tried to escape this past year. That thought left me with much heavier steps than when I began my walk.

seven

I CAME around the side of the house and was startled by someone standing at the front door. There were two pieces of gray luggage at the bottom of the steps. The shadows created by the porch overhang hid the person except for the bottom half of their legs, legs that definitely belonged to a woman. Was Nate's mystery guest a woman? That notion pinched at my chest.

"Hello?" I said cautiously.

The person swung around, and sunlight lit her face.

"Mom?"

"Annie-poo, there you are!" Mom lifted her arms as if she was going to bestow one of her rare hugs on me. I knew better. She just as quickly lowered them. "Be a dear and get my suitcases. They were too heavy for me. My knees are bad. Doctor says I might even need to replace one." My mom had always been quite vain. She kept her hair dyed the same rusty auburn, even though I knew, for a fact, every strand beneath the hair color was gray. She also loved to get Botox injections. Judging by the stiffness of her face, it seemed probable that she'd recently had a few. Cora and I had no real idea how old our mom was. She refused to tell us. At her birthday parties we were required to put four candles, one for each season of the year, on her cake. My dad was sixty-nine, and they got married in their early twenties, so my best guess would be that Rhonda St. James was around that same age. Although, if she kept up with the hair dye and Botox, she'd soon be looking more like my sister than my mom.

"I wasn't expecting you," I said, trying not to sound impolite, and at the same time, letting her know that she should have given me a heads up. I picked up her bags. They were heavy, but that didn't necessarily mean a long stay. Like Cora, Mom tended to overdress for every situation. Even now, for the mostly rough and very rustic ferry ride to the island, she'd put on shiny high heels and a fur trimmed coat. I knew without asking that she wouldn't stay long. My mom usually found the island too confining. Her visits were always short.

My arms were laden with luggage, which eliminated the possibility of a hug altogether. I leaned in to kiss her cheek. Her hand went up. "Oh, not that side, Annie-poo. It's tender from—well—from my last—uh, dental appointment."

"All right, you had two Annie-poos. No more please." As far as I was concerned, she got one opportunity for a kiss and she missed it. I didn't bother with the other cheek, and I also held back the deserved eye roll about the *dental appointment*. There I was, on the porch for all of ten seconds with my mom, and I was already feeling like an annoyed teenager.

40

"Cora told me she was working today. That's so disappointing," she said as we stepped inside.

"So, Cora knew you were coming for a visit?" I asked.

"Why, yes, I told her last Friday. Didn't she mention it?"

"Mom!" Cora trotted down the stairs. Her skinny jeans were, perhaps, a bit too skinny and her heels too spiky for a race down the flight of stairs. I held my breath until she safely reached the landing.

The hug for Cora was exuberant but quick. "Cora, my little beauty, did you get the email about Rodney Dinkley? He's perfect, right? And he owns a massive yacht. He sails to Europe once a year."

"Mom, I don't think I can marry a man with the last name Dinkley."

And, there it was. I'd fallen into a world that only Cora and Rhonda could create, a world so shallow, fish could not survive, and a world so silly, even circus clowns refused to step in it.

Mom was obviously working hard behind the scenes to get Cora back into a lifestyle where diamonds hung in clusters like grapes and the family boat was larger than a small town. And Cora's only reason for not considering this latest match was that he had a quirky last name.

"How long are you staying?" It was the only question in my head.

"Oh, I don't know, dear. Could I get that guest room that has a view of the ocean?"

"None of my rooms have a view of the ocean," I said dryly.

Mom tapped her chin. "Are you sure about that? I distinctly remember a room with an ocean view."

"I think I'd remember if I had a room with an ocean view, but I've got one with a river view. It'll have to do." I badly wanted to mention that the Frostfall Hotel had a lot of ocean view rooms, but I kept it to myself. I picked up the luggage again. "I'll carry these up to the room. Cora, why don't you start the coffeepot?"

"Oh, wait, Annie—'" She refrained from adding on the poo ending. It was probably the best I could hope for. She'd used the humiliating nickname all my life. When I was little, it didn't bother me, but it quickly became a major embarrassment, especially when she used it in front of my teenage friends. For Cora, it was my beautiful princess and other sparkly nicknames, but for Anna, it was Annie-poo. Mom took hold of one of her suitcases. She laid it flat, opened it and pulled out a photo album. "I kept myself busy all winter taking care of one of the things on my bucket list. Putting my many photographs into an album. I thought we girls could look through it over coffee."

Cora clapped excitedly. "I love looking at old pictures." Of course she did because she never took a bad photo in her life. Even her baby photos looked as if they were created just for a baby food commercial. Mine, on the other hand, were less than flattering. I had dark hair and a somewhat misshapen head. Sometimes it was hard to believe that Cora and I came from the same womb. I was sure Mom thought that all the time.

Mom snapped shut the luggage, pulled it upright and

42

handed it unceremoniously off to me as if I was the bellboy in a hotel. My tip was going to be suffering the humiliation of being called Annie-poo in front of my housemates, and one housemate, in particular.

I realized as I pushed the luggage into the larger of the two guest rooms that both of my spare rooms would be occupied. There was definitely no more space at the house this week. I was going to need to bring some chairs out of storage for the dining table, and now I was worried I didn't have enough food for everyone. I hadn't planned for two extra mouths at the table.

By the time I landed back downstairs, the smell of coffee and the sound of my mom and sister laughing replaced some of the grumpy, woe is me stuff with fond nostalgia. Mom and Cora had not waited for me to start on the album. It was fine. I knew without looking that Cora's photos, including her two magnificent six-figure weddings, would take up most of the pages. (There I was doing it again. Darn those old habits.)

I poured myself a cup and sat down on the other side of my mom. She had the album splayed open in front of her. She'd added in little handwritten notes and stickers to go with the pictures. "Remember this?" Mom asked with a laugh.

I glanced at the photo. It was twelve-year-old me with a mouthful of new braces and wearing the proper amount of misery to go with it.

Cora laughed. "You did not like wearing those braces." Naturally, Cora had been born with a Hollywood starlet's smile. No braces needed.

"I don't think you'll find one kid on this planet who enjoys wearing a mouthful of train tracks, train tracks that don't allow you to eat taffy apples, caramel corn, gummi bears or any of the other foods that delight teenagers."

"But your teeth turned out so pretty," Mom said.

"I had to talk around wearing a bulky retainer throughout high school," I reminded her. Not to mention, the second I stopped wearing the thing my teeth worked their hardest to shift back to the position nature had given them.

We sipped coffee over some of the most lavish, professionally staged wedding pictures ever printed on paper. In each one, Cora looked like a painting and her groom looked like a readymade Halloween prop. But my mom and sister didn't take notice of the two terrible, old men standing at the end of each of her grand bridal entrances. They were only interested in the bride.

"Oh look, Annie," Mom said. "You looked so pretty in that peach chiffon Maid of Honor dress." I occasionally earned the word pretty, but it was handed out sparingly.

Cora flipped the page. "Here's your wedding, Anna." She looked up at me with worry. "Is it all right? Maybe we should skip this page."

"No, it's fine." I'd pulled out Michael's and my wedding photos one time about three years after his absence, but I hadn't looked at them since.

I was relieved to find that I could look at Michael now and not instantly break into tears. Michael was almost a head taller than me, even in my heels. I'd picked a simple silky dress with long sleeves and a flowing skirt. The low-cut décolletage was rimmed with opal beads.

"Oh, sis, you looked so lovely that day. And Michael looked dashing in his tuxedo." Cora leaned closer to the album to survey a photo of our twenty-plus wedding guests sitting at round tables. "Oh, there I am. I look lovely too." She leaned closer and pressed her finger against the plastic covering. "Who is that woman standing next to the dance area wearing a very serious, scrutinizing look? I don't remember her, and your guest list was so small."

Mom leaned closer and adjusted her reading glasses. "I don't remember her either." She straightened. "My, what a sourpuss."

I pulled the album closer and took a good look at the photo. They were right. The woman looked dead serious or angry. It was hard to tell which one. She had straight blonde hair, blue eyes, a button nose and a mouth that didn't fit the rest of her fairy tale princess appearance. It was a stern mouth, slathered in red lipstick. Something about her reminded me of Joan Crawford, beautiful but hard.

"Well?" Mom asked. "Who is that woman?"

"I have no idea. Maybe she came with the caterer," I suggested.

"But they all wore uniforms. This woman is wearing a flouncy dress and glittery earrings as if she's a guest."

What Cora said made sense. She didn't fit in as someone working at the venue or putting out food. I looked at the picture again. A small, inexplicable shiver ran through me. There was something almost familiar about the woman, and yet, I couldn't, for the life of me, say who she was. And as Cora had so typically Cora pointed out, we had a very small guest list. I knew everyone on it.

"Maybe she's one of those wedding crashers," Mom said. "Like the movie."

I nodded. "Let's move on. I've got to start lunch. Besides, it doesn't really matter now." And it didn't matter. The dashing groom, the intimate wedding and even the mysterious sour-faced wedding guest were long gone.

eight

I LOVED MY SISTER. I loved my mom. Together, I could only take them in small doses. Something about my mom always brought out the syrupy, shallow side of my sister. Suddenly, she was that woman again, the one whose only life goal was to marry for money and live a posh lifestyle befitting any American princess. After a lunch, where I discovered the true magic of obnoxious Quentin Oxley through his sublime sourdough bread, I took Huck out for a brisk walk. Opal had come down for lunch and a short chat with my mom before retiring back to her room. Our walk had left her sore and exhausted. I blamed myself. I'd pushed her too far for her first real hike. She'd already taken a long nap, so another sleepless night was ahead of her.

Huck picked up a gallop as we turned the first bend on Calico Trail. The dog barked excitedly as he ran ahead. I soon found out it wasn't a squirrel that had caught his attention.

Nate was just stepping off the boardwalk. A man with a little less height and shoulder width walked next to him. He had a big backpack hanging casually off one shoulder of his worn bomber jacket. His hands were stuffed into the pockets of his faded jeans. His hair was lighter and thinner than Nate's, and he had big dark eyes and a sort of cocky tilt to his mouth that looked like a permanent grin.

Nate's smile splashed white as he spotted Huck and then me. He waved and the two men set to work giving the dog a proper greeting. I reached them just as Nate was telling his friend one of his many tales of adventure with Huck. It always made me smile to hear him talk so lovingly about the dog.

"Anna, this is my friend, Arlo. Arlo, this is Anna."

The cocky tilt remained, and it was more charming up close. "Ah, so this is the famous Anna." He took my hand between his and smiled. "So glad to finally meet you." I was at a disadvantage. Nate never talked about people from his past, but it seemed information had flowed the other direction.

"Well, I'm hardly famous, but I do make chocolate chip cookies that are worthy of an award."

"I can vouch for that." Nate patted his stomach.

Arlo patted it too and laughed. "Seems to me the last time I saw you, Nate, there wasn't quite so much of you."

"Hey, I've still got the old six-pack," Nate argued. "Some of the cans are dented, but they're still there." Nate turned back to me. "Arlo texted that he got on the earlier ferry, so I took the afternoon off to meet him," Nate explained. "Where are you two headed?" He patted Huck's head. Huck hadn't taken his shiny brown eyes off Nathaniel.

"I'm just out getting some fresh air. My mom is here." I added a smile that only Nate could interpret. We were already at that place in our relationship.

"Were you expecting her?"

"Nope. Apparently, she told Cora, and Cora didn't feel the need to tell me."

"If I'm in the way, I could get a room at the hotel," Arlo said with a thumb over his shoulder.

"No, you're not in the way. I happen to have two guest rooms, although I have to warn you that my mom already snagged the one with the ocean view." I turned to head back to the house with them.

Nate scratched his head. "Which room has an ocean view?" he asked.

"None of them. But Mom insisted on that one."

Arlo laughed. "I see our moms came from the same mold."

Huck trotted next to us for awhile before getting distracted by three chickadees searching for seeds under a shrub. The birds were coming back to the island, and soon my dog and his short attention span would be zigzagging back and forth across the trail to chase everything that moved.

"How do you two know each other?" I asked.

"I'm his twin," Arlo said.

My face snapped his direction. "Just kidding. I wish I saw that when I looked in the mirror." He leaned his head toward Nathaniel.

"We were on the force together," Nate said.

"But I was never on homicide," Arlo added. "Far too many dead bodies."

I laughed. I'd only known him a few minutes, but I already liked Nate's friend.

"Are you on vacation?" I asked. It was just small talk, that, and I wanted to know if there was any other reason for Arlo's visit, like trying to lure Nate back to his old position on the force. Nate had left his dream job behind because of one failed case, albeit it a *big* case. A serial killer had been stalking the city for the last eight years. The murders were usually a good distance apart, and thus far, the evidence had been thin. Nate had been in charge of the team tasked with hunting down the maniac, but the team had failed. When the monster struck again this winter, it nearly wiped away all the progress Nate had made while living and working on the island. It was a stark reminder that his failure to catch the killer meant another innocent victim was dead, brutally stabbed to death in her own bed.

Arlo stooped down to pick up a long gray feather. A seagull feather, judging by the length and color. He twirled it in his fingers. "I'm in between jobs."

"So you've left law enforcement too?" I realized I'd worded the question badly when I spotted Nate staring down at the ground as we walked.

"I should," Arlo sighed. He tossed aside the feather. It

floated back and forth before landing between the stalks of a yarrow plant. "Especially when I see how relaxed and happy my buddy here looks. I've decided to dig my heels deeper into the mud by joining the feds."

"The feds? You mean the FBI?"

"That's right. It was something I dreamed about as a kid. I'm heading up to D.C. for training after I leave here."

Nate had sort of extricated himself from the conversation by pretending to be enamored with the scenery, scenery he saw every day. His sudden lack of engagement was saying a lot. Again, we were at that point in our relationship where I could immediately sense something was wrong. Other than finding myself, involuntarily, as the island's top *detective*, I knew little about law enforcement, but I always imagined that moving from city detective into the secretive and highly official land of the Federal Bureau of Investigations was like, to put it in Cora's terms, moving from the title of Miss Teen Tallahassee to Miss Universe.

"That's wonderful. Congratulations," I said with not nearly enough enthusiasm. I was toning it down for Nate's sake. I was reading something on his face. It might have been envy, but I was sure if I gave it further thought, I'd come to the conclusion that it was regret. Was Arlo's arrival going to make Nate regret his decision to live on Frostfall Island? His friend and coworker was moving up in the law enforcement chain. He'd soon be wearing an FBI badge, and Nate was carrying a metal lunch pail after a day hammering nails and laying bricks. He said he loved working with his hands and being out on the coast all day, but I knew, without question, that he often thought about his old life. Arlo's arrival was going to bring all those memories back with fresh new clarity.

Suddenly, that sourdough bread was sitting in my stomach like a lump of raw dough.

nine

DINNER WAS CROWDED, loud and interesting. Interesting could never be avoided if you sat down with a group of people who were so different in every way that it was hard to believe they were part of the same species. Winston sat mostly quiet, in his millennial bubble, eating his vegetable lasagna and watching as the forty plus crowd chatted about those horrid cords on phones, the fact that we had no dating apps to meet people so you had to choose from a small circle of people who were near you in proximity, and that TikTok was just the sound your grandmother's annoying mantle clock made when you were spending the night at her house. Even Tobias joined in on the trip to the past. He told us that the grandparents who raised him had grown up during the Great Depression, and they'd never changed their ways, even long after the economy recovered. His grandmother saved everything. They had a collection of ketchup packets enough for a year's worth of fries. And Gran, as Tobias called her, had to light the stove to cook because the notion of buying a newfangled appliance like one with an automatic pilot light was a waste of money. Opal kept some of her more outlandish musings, namely tales from her days as Rudy Valentino, to herself, but she joined right in with nostalgic stories from her childhood. Her father was rather progressive, and they were the first family on the block to own a microwave. She said the entire neighborhood came to watch a slice of cheese being melted on bread. It was the talk of her small town for days.

I was glad to see Nathaniel's rather pensive mood had lightened as he joined in on the conversation and laughter. Arlo was one of those lively, attractive people who could pull all the energy his direction. He'd certainly pulled my sister's attention his way. She barely took her eyes off him all night. In turn, my mom barely took her eyes off my sister. Only instead of the flirty smile plastered across Cora's face, Mom wore a disapproving glower. I hadn't had time to fill my mom and sister in on the fact that Arlo would be an agent for the FBI. Cora would probably like that. She liked strong, dangerous types almost as much as she liked halfway to the grave billionaires, but my mom would not be impressed. The only things that impressed Mom were twelve figure bank accounts, never mind if the man was on oxygen and using a walker to get around. Money was all that counted. As far as my mom knew, Nate was just a boarder. She didn't notice the sparks between us (or maybe only I saw them) and I was fine keeping it that way. Mom had little interest in my love life. And while most of her friends were already knee deep in grandchildren, my mom was just as happy to keep the age-affirming term grandmother off her title list.

After the loud, boisterous meal, Huck plopped down on his kitchen pillow with an exhausted sigh. Arlo and Nate had decided the heavy meal was best followed with an evening walk. Nate was anxious to show Arlo the lighthouse. That helped alleviate some of my earlier worry. If he was excited to show off his construction project, then maybe he wasn't having the big regrets I'd imagined. Cora, who would rather poke her eye out with a fork than take a meaningless stroll around the island, was suddenly keen for the exercise. Arlo didn't seem disappointed about her going along. He'd had what I'd termed a Cora-filled gaze on his face almost the second we'd walked into the house and found my gorgeous sister sitting at the table in a skin tight knit dress and pearl drop earrings. Even when my sister was going casual, and by casual, I meant less diamonds and makeup, she still looked stunning. Arlo had done everything but trip over his tongue when he saw her. My mom was far too tired for a walk, but she could possibly drag along to see the lighthouse (her words). I knew she was planning to keep a watchful eye on her daughter as if Cora was just sixteen going out on a first date. She was tagging along as a protective chaperone. In the end, my suggestion that Mom take along a flashlight to avoid wrenching an ankle or stepping on one of the many night critters crisscrossing the trails changed her mind. She went up for a hot bath and early bed, but she managed to pull Cora aside for a private chat. I didn't need to be a fly on the wall to know what they were talking about.

The walk sounded nice, but I'd been out and about so much during the day, I'd fallen behind on my meal prep, and now I had a bigger guest list for breakfast. I decided potato hash and scrambled eggs would be just the thing, and the only way I could pull that off was to cut the potatoes, onions and peppers ahead of time. I'd turned on my favorite playlist. Van Morrison was crooning softly through the little portable kitchen speaker as I sliced my way through four pounds of potatoes, three onions and three peppers. I was deep into the rhythm of my vegetable cutting symphony when the back steps creaked with heavy footsteps.

Huck lifted his head but was too tired to get up, even for Nate.

"You're back faster than I expected," I said as I continued to chop.

"Got them as far as the lighthouse. Arlo was more interested in your sister than the work I was doing."

"Don't take it to heart. There is little that can steal a man's attention better than Cora Cromwell. Not even a century-plus old lighthouse that is bursting with grace, history and charm."

"I thought they might prefer to be alone," Nate said.

I stopped the knife and looked up. "You left them at the lighthouse?"

"I figured Cora knew the way back."

I laughed. "You might have been overestimating my sister, but you're right, I'm sure they'll manage. It's not that big of an island."

"No, it's not." Nate poured himself a splash of the wine

we'd had at dinner and leaned his hip against the counter next to me. I sensed some of the solemn mood had returned. I was sure it wasn't about Arlo's lack of interest in the lighthouse.

I had three mounds of vegetables, plenty for the morning hash. I followed his lead and poured myself a bit of wine. I picked up the photo album that Mom had left on my kitchen desk and sat down at the table. "Want to see some old photos? You'll soon see that my sister has never had an ugly day in her life, while I've had more than my share of them."

Nate pulled his chair closer to mine, leaned over and kissed me, leaving the sweet taste of wine on my lips. "You need to stop that," he said.

"Stop what?" I asked, knowing full well what he meant. I blamed my new phase of feeling troll-ish next to my sister on Mom's arrival.

"Your sister is very beautiful, but she doesn't have what you have."

"And what is that?" I asked with a smile and lifted my hand. "Hands that smell like onions?"

He took hold of my hand and kissed each knuckle tenderly. "You've got a soul that's so deep and so incredible, your sister could never hope to compete with it."

I kissed him back. "Sorry if I'm seeming pathetic. My mom brings that out in me. But you know what? I'm done having my ugly duckling moment. There's nothing Rhonda can do to spoil that. I've become the swan. You made me that swan."

"Nope. You were always a swan."

We kissed again. We so rarely had time alone, it was nice to have the kitchen to ourselves. I gazed at him. His navy blue eyes looked the color of the ocean under the kitchen lights.

"I like your friend, Arlo," I said. I was hoping he'd open up about how he was feeling, but it wasn't to be. Sometimes, he was an open book, and other times, the cover was shut tight.

Nate relaxed back. His long legs were lightly tangled with mine. "Yeah, he's a character. I'm happy for him. Back when we were rookies together, he always talked about working for the FBI. Now he's going to achieve that dream." It seemed he was only going to talk about his friend's ladder climb but not how he felt about it. Nate leaned forward and flipped the book open. It landed on a page where Cora and I were dressed for an aunt's wedding. Cora was only thirteen or fourteen. She was clad in a sugary confection of delicate lace and buttery chiffon. After the divorce, it seemed both my parents struggled financially. Life had been much more solid when they were together. But even with the constant "tightening of our belts" as Mom used to say, there was always magical hidden money somewhere (mostly credit cards) for pretty clothes for my sister. My mom counted on Cora's beauty to pull us out of our penny pinching lifestyle, so she considered it an investment in the family future.

Nate pointed at me in the photo. "You're so cute." He smiled. The photos had been a good diversion. "You don't look happy."

"I hated weddings. I'm still not a big fan. Too much idle, awkward chitchat. And, as I recall, on that particular

Saturday some of my school friends were taking a trip to the beach, but I had to go to my aunt's wedding in an itchy dress."

"Your sister looks happy."

"Yes, weddings are her favorite thing in the world. Especially if she's the one wearing white."

A few page flips later, past a couple awkward, braces-filled teen photos that made me seriously wonder why I thought opening the photo album was a good idea, we were at my wedding photos.

Nate stared at the picture for awhile. "How can you not see it?" he asked.

I leaned forward to look at the picture again. "I don't know how I missed her. I don't know who she is."

Nate looked up confused. "What? No. I mean how can you not see that you were always a swan. Look at you—in that dress... You look incredible."

My face warmed with a blush. "Thank you. I did love that dress."

"Michael looks happy. I'll bet that was the best day of his life," Nate said. "Who were you talking about? This rather stern looking woman in the background?" He pointed at the photo.

"Yes, it's the strangest thing. Mom, Cora and I were looking at the album. I don't remember seeing her at the wedding and it was small. I have no idea who she is. I probably wouldn't have noticed her at all except she looks very angry. She's a mystery and yet something about her seems familiar. Oh well, enough trips down memory lane this evening. I've got to put my veggies in the refrigerator. Do you and Arlo have plans tomorrow, or do you have to work?"

"I took the day off. Not sure what we're going to be up to. It's not as if there's a long list of things to do on Frostfall Island."

That was probably the last thing I needed to hear at the end of the evening. Now I'd be tossing and turning all night, worrying that Nate would follow his friend off the island to return to civilization.

ten

MY PREDICTION WAS RIGHT. I couldn't sleep. I turned on a light and sat up to read, hoping a few chapters would lull me into sleepiness. After a page, where I had to reread every sentence and mentally tell myself to pay attention to the words, there was a soft knock on the door.

I pushed on my slippers and tossed a robe over my shoulders. My mom stood in the semi dark hallway wearing an extra plush hot pink robe. She was never good at rubbing in her nightly cold cream, so there were greasy white spots all over her face.

"Mom? What's wrong?"

"Couldn't sleep." She looked past me into the room. "Can I come in, or are we going to talk with me standing out in this drafty hallway?"

"Sure, come inside."

Mom plodded across the room in shiny silver slippers. She made herself comfortable on the far side of the bed. She was quite the sight in her hot pink, silver combo. She crossed her arms and surveyed the room. "This room is so much bigger than the guest room." There was just enough crispness in her tone to let me know I should have given her the biggest room. For a woman who struggled financially for most of her life, she never failed in her attempt to be a spoiled princess.

"That's because this is the master bedroom," I reminded her.

"Oh my, am I sitting on Michael's side of the bed?"

I sat down on my side. "It's all right, Mom." Even though, it sort of wasn't. No one ever sat on that side of the bed except, occasionally, Huck. "What's been keeping you up? Room not comfortable enough? Too small? Lack of an ocean view?" I couldn't sleep either, but it didn't mean I wasn't tired and part of that had been due to my mom's unexpected visit.

Mom tapped my arm. "Stop being so snide. I just thought the house had an ocean view. After all, it's a small island, and it's surrounded by ocean. How did Michael manage to buy a house that had no view?"

"He didn't buy it. It was an inheritance, remember? And I happen to think it's the best house with the best location on the island."

"Yes, it's very nice. Big and roomy." She pulled her robe closed. "But a little drafty too."

"I think that's what someone can expect with a very old house. It would be far more drafty if it overlooked the ocean," I added for good measure. "Why couldn't you sleep?" I asked.

"I'm concerned about your sister."

"Cora is perfectly happy here on the island. We're still close as ever, and I like having her here too."

Mom made a clucking sound. "She'll never reach her full potential on Frosty Island."

"It's Frostfall Island, and you're talking about her like she's eighteen with her big adult years still ahead of her. Cora tried the billionaire's wife trick twice, and both times it failed. The husbands died, and their past families, something you have to expect when you marry a man in his nineties, swept in and left her with an impractical wardrobe and a few nice pieces of jewelry. Cora is working, holding down her first job, which, as I say it aloud, is comical. She likes working at the tea shop, and the customers adore her."

"Of course they do. I mean she stands out like a shiny star on this dreary little island."

My teeth gritted, and I sensed that I was going to have an even harder time falling asleep after her visit. "This dreary island is my home, and those of us who don't shine like stars are quite content here."

Mom reached over and patted my arm somewhat patronizingly. "I didn't mean that you don't shine like a star, Anna. You do—in your own way."

I'd had enough of our mother daughter chat. "Well, Mom, it's been wonderful talking to you. I probably can still hold off on that therapy for another month or two, so I have a chance to absorb this visit."

"Annie-poo, you're angry."

"Nope and adding in my ridiculous childhood nickname is not going to make anything about this chat endearing. I've also figured out the motive for your visit. You came here hoping to talk Cora back to the mainland. Why don't you let her decide what to do with her life?"

"I might ask you the same thing." Mom swung her legs around and stood up from the bed. "You're cranky because it's late. You always got grumpy when it was past your bedtime."

"Ah ha, thanks so much for the visit, Mom, and let me know if you need an extra blanket." I was hurrying her to the door before I said something I'd regret. If only my mom had those same safety measures in place in her head.

"Good night, dear. Get some sleep because crankiness makes your forehead wrinkle. Those lines will become permanent if you don't take care." With that, I snapped shut the door.

I paced the floor a few times, hoping to work off the sharp edge my mom had left me with. I didn't know how I could have missed it—her hidden motive. Mom was having a tough time accepting that Cora was stuck on our *dreary* little island and missing a potential third marriage with an old and decaying billionaire. I was sure the photo album was part of the plan. Show Cora the glamorous wedding pictures and lure my sister back for a third round.

I paced the room again and stared at the slight dent my mom had left on Michael's side of the bed. Something about the sight of the concave quilt and mattress triggered a memory. Michael and I would sit in bed on cold nights and talk about our childhoods and our teenage years. From all accounts, Michael was sort of a *big man* on campus type, football star, popular all around. It wasn't surprising to me. One particularly stormy night, when the wind roared across the island so fiercely the whole house shook, Michael and I sat in bed with hot tea reminiscing about the past. He decided to dig out his high school yearbook.

"The woman in the photo," I muttered as I hurried to the closet. I'd given away most of Michael's clothes and shoes, but a few of his more personal belongings were stored in a box at the back of the closet. I leaned down, pushed through my hanging clothes and reached past my line of shoes. It took a good stretch to get ahold of the box, a large shoebox that once held my first pair of galoshes for life on the island. They'd come in handy once I realized that Frostfall was far too rugged and filled with nature for the sensible shoes I wore during my days in business. I dragged the heavy box out from the corner and sat back on my knees in front of the closet. I took a deep breath and opened the lid. Two of Michael's favorite pipes sat on top of his leather-bound captain's log. Several years ago, they were items that would draw out instant tears, but I could look at them now without falling apart.

I carefully pushed aside the pipes. The faint aroma of his favorite tobacco spiraled up toward my nose. His high school yearbook was at the bottom. It was a big, unwieldy book with a dark blue and gold embossed cover. A flutter of nerves went through me as I opened the book. Inside were all the handwritten messages of good luck and have a great summer and all the mundane things we write in each other's year-books. I flipped through to the middle of the book where some of the extracurricular photos had been placed by the yearbook team. I paused to smile at the photo of Michael in his football uniform. He was wearing a big smile on top of massive shoulder pads and the number 16 on his jersey.

The messages and sports photos had not sent me into the farthest depths of my cluttered closet. It was something else, a picture just a few pages past the athletic teams and cheer squad. I passed by the most likely to succeed, best smile and most likely to become president page and stopped at the cutest couple photo. Michael and his high school sweetheart had been voted cutest couple. He'd laughed out loud when he showed me the picture. Naturally, my first question at the time had been what happened to Denise Fengarten? That was the name of the petite brunette he had tucked under his arm in the photo. Michael had said Denise was too clingy. He broke up with her a year after they graduated. That was all he'd said about her.

I stared at the photo a long time, long enough to send a chill through me that had nothing to do with the drafty house. It was her. The hair color had changed, but I knew, without a doubt, that Denise Fengarten was the scowling mystery woman in my wedding photo. She was not on the guest list. In fact, the only time I'd heard her name was that stormy night when Michael and I browsed through his yearbook. He never mentioned her again. So, the big question was—how on earth did she end up at our wedding?

I closed the book and placed it back in the box. I had a long, sleepless night ahead of me.

eleven

IT WAS WELL before sunrise when I headed out with my paints. I'd only slept a couple hours, but I could usually get through the day with just a few hours sleep. Tonight, I'd fall into bed like a lead ball. My only worry was that I'd fall asleep during movie night. Considering I was the unofficial hostess of the event, that wouldn't look too good. I was regretting putting it on the calendar. There were just too many frets and fears bouncing around in my head to be able to concentrate on setting up an enjoyable movie night. My mom's late night chat had only added to my worries. She was here to talk Cora off the island. Rhonda had made that all too clear last night. Cora would make up her own mind. I'd be sad if she left, but I'd manage to keep it together. I wasn't quite as sure about Nate's possible departure. Not that he'd said anything about leaving. We'd had a nice, flirty few moments alone in the kitchen, and he never brought up leaving. But then, would he? Surely, it wouldn't be something he'd just blurt out. He knew it would be hard for me to hear.

There was still enough darkness shrouding the island that my big, brave dog stuck close to my side. He never liked to wander off when there were still more shadows than skittering mice and squirrels. If I gave it some thought, it was still too dark to find a subject for my watercolors. Even the bright orange milkweed and brilliant pink seaside peas were keeping their heads down in the shadowy light. I wasn't entirely sure I'd get anything of worth out of my paintbrushes anyhow. My head was heavy from tossing and turning all night and thinking too hard about the possible changes coming my way. Lights from the wharf and marina pulled Huck and me toward them like moths. The smooth boardwalk was a much better choice when there was little to light our way. Huck felt more comfortable when we reached the area of the island that was just starting to buzz with activity.

Fishing boats were firing up their motors, sending a diesel scented ruckus across the wharf. Frannie's husband was mopping the deck on the *Salty Bottom* as the engine warmed up for the first trip across the harbor. I'd exchanged a few texts with Fran and discovered her sore throat had morphed inconveniently into a head cold. She confided that she was just as happy to have a few days off the water, especially with the bustling summer tourist season looming in the not too distant future.

Huck and I walked briskly. The early morning air had a

snap to it. It was exactly what I needed to wake up fully. I had breakfast to cook for a crew of people, and I needed my wits about me.

Huck lifted his head as a large figure riding at top speed on a bicycle came toward us. As the rider drew closer, I recognized, first, his broad shouldered silhouette and then his face and thick red hair. It was Jamie Baxter. He pedaled hard as if he was racing for his life, but there was no one behind him. He should have been out on his boat already, but it seemed he had more important matters than fishing to deal with.

I waved as he rode past, but he stared ahead with laser sharpness. I had an inkling about where he might be headed. I decided to follow. I had enough to deal with this week. I certainly didn't need a murder on my hands. Not that I considered polite, shy Jamie the murdering type, but the new baker seemed to have made it his mission to anger everyone on the island. Everyone, that was, except Remi Seymour, Jamie's steady girlfriend.

Considering that Jamie was riding his bicycle as if he was competing in the Tour de France, Huck and I had to pick up our pace considerably. We were both breathing hard by the time we reached the bakery. The doors weren't open yet, and surprisingly, no one had ventured out in the darkness to get in line for a chocolate croissant. The aroma filled steam coming from the vents assured me Quentin had been inside for hours baking his wondrous creations.

Jamie had already tossed his bike aside. It was on the

ground directly in front of the bakery. I tapped Huck's head to stop his progress. His nose was twitching as he trotted straight toward the wonderful smells. He looked back at me and turned to see why I, too, wasn't heading toward the delicious smells. I motioned for him to sit, and we stayed in the shadow of Jack's restaurant awning. Jamie had his face and hands pressed against the glass on the front door of the bakery. His heavy breathing caused the glass to fog. He wiped it angrily with the sleeve of his coat.

Jamie knocked hard on the glass door. It shook all the windows.

"Oxley!" he yelled. "I know you're in there. Open and up and face me like a man." His fist pounded the glass again. "Oxley!"

There were few people out yet. Jack wasn't at the restaurant. It was far too early.

Jamie pounded the glass and shook the door wildly. The glass windows vibrated. From my vantage point, it was hard to see inside the bakery, but a light went on. I leaned out farther to get a better view. If Oxley opened the door, I might be witness to a fight or worse. My adrenaline was up. Huck seemed to sense trouble too.

Quentin had come out from his kitchen. He was holding a long serrated bread cutting knife.

"Coward," Jamie yelled. "Open up. The only weapons I have are these." He held up his meaty fists.

"Leave my premises or I'll call the police," Oxley yelled through the glass. It seemed Quentin was still new enough

to the island that he didn't know about our police department, the one that didn't exist. Something told me lazy
Detective Norwich wasn't going to make the *arduous* journey
to his least favorite island to deal with a dispute between a
fisherman and a baker.

As I visualized what that might look like, a flicker of
movement caught my eye. It seemed we weren't alone on the
boardwalk, after all. Someone was standing well past the
bakery mirroring my own position by hiding in the shadows
of the museum. Sunlight had started as a whisper across the
island. I couldn't make out anything except the silhouette of
a fairly tall figure, a man it seemed, standing with a dark hat
pulled low over his head and the tall collars of his coat acting
as a shield for his face. My guess would be that the man was
trying to hide from the people at the bakery door.

It seemed the two men facing down each other through
the bakery door had reached an impasse. They stared at each
other through the fogged up glass, Jamie with his fists
clenched, and Quentin with his big ugly knife. After a few
tense moments, Jamie raised his finger and pointed it at the
baker. "You'd better watch your back, Oxley." He turned
around, snatched up his bike so fast it lifted off the ground
and then bounced as the tires hit the cement. He climbed on
the bicycle and rode off. He was too filled with rage to notice
me nosing around in the dark. Which reminded me about the
mystery watcher on the other side of the bakery. A thin
stream of daylight gave me a touch more courage. I stepped
out from under the awning and made it seem as if I was just

heading that direction naturally. The man dashed between the buildings. By the time I reached the museum, he was gone, and I wasn't about to go chasing him. The rising sun reminded me that I had a breakfast to cook.

"Come on, Huck. It's been quite an adventurous outing."

twelve

ASIDE from nearly forgetting to add salt to my potato hash, the breakfast turned out well. (I wasn't feeling too confident after my lack of sleep.) Winston hurried his meal to get to work, and, I suspected, to free himself from another round of conversation about the *good ole days*. Toby unexpectedly took his breakfast to go. It seemed he'd had enough of the big crowd at the table, and Nate's friend, Arlo, had an extra big presence. Nate, on the other hand, was especially quiet.

Arlo and Cora were laughing wildly about something. I'd lost the thread of conversation while packing up Tobias' breakfast and lunch. I sat down next to Nate who was nursing his cup of coffee like it was life support. Mom was scowling at my sister and Arlo in such a way that it was almost laughable.

I elbowed Nate lightly. "Penny for your thoughts," I said, for lack of a better conversation starter.

The line that I liked so much on the side of his mouth

deepened. "Not worth the penny. I'm just tired, I guess." He leaned closer to whisper. "I forgot how exhausting Arlo could be. He had us up at the crack of dawn doing push-ups and sit-ups. He needs to train for his new job."

"I thought I heard an inordinate amount of creaking coming from the upstairs. Is that something you ever thought about?" I asked. The lack of sleep was making me blurt out stupid things.

Nate stared at the cup of coffee nestled between his hands. His long lashes dropped down, and he grew quiet for a moment. "Not going to lie. I'm a little jealous. Working with the feds always seemed like a cool step up the ladder."

It was not the answer I hoped to hear.

Our conversation stopped because Arlo's and Cora's had grown so loud it would be hard to hear each other. "Cora, milady, I can't believe you're sitting here on this little island. You should be on a Hollywood movie set."

It was a line my sister had heard too often, and I was sure she wouldn't be impressed by its lack of originality. I was wrong. She tapped him hard on the chest. "Arlo, honey, that is so sweet of you to say." Her diamond watch glittered as she smoothed her hair back behind one ear. There was already not a hair out of place, but it was her go-to move when in flirt mode and she was in major flirt mode. My mom, on the other hand, looked positively apoplectic.

Opal sat quietly eating her breakfast and watching the various scenes at the table as if she was sitting behind a big vat of popcorn at the theater.

Arlo finally pulled his undivided attention away from

Cora. "Well, Nate, ole buddy, are we going to head out and see the sights? You mentioned something about a bike ride around the island. That'd be good." He patted his stomach. "After all of Anna's delicious cooking, I'm going to show up at the Bureau with a spare tire. I've still got a lot of training to do to pass that physical. A bike ride is just what I need."

Nate shrugged and half smiled. "Don't expect it to be too grueling. The path around the island is easy enough for summer tourists." Nate stood up. There was definitely an air of disappointment in his posture. Arlo's visit was making him rethink his most recent life changing decisions, and the fact that his life change just happened to include me wasn't going to make much difference. I sensed some heartbreak coming my way, and I had only myself to blame.

thirteen

ONCE THE HOUSE HAD CLEARED, with Cora off to a job
that was now on the ropes because of the competing bakery,
Mom upstairs reading, Opal back to her room to catch up on
all the movies she'd missed while out on a walk the morning
before and Nate and his boisterous buddy out on the bicycles, I decided I was in need of a long chat with my favorite
ear lender, Olive Everhart. I packed a basket with some leftover potato hash, a bowl of fresh strawberries and some
sweet potato biscuits I'd pulled from the freezer. They were
delicious slathered with soft honey butter, so I whipped up a
batch of the creamy goodness and put it in a small jar.

The heavy basket swinging from my arm signaled to Huck
that we were heading to Olive's cottage and, subsequently, to
Olive's treat jar. He raced ahead, barking occasionally, I
assumed to let the wildlife hiding in the shrubs know he had
no time to menace them this morning because his favorite
cookies awaited him.

Huck reached the house before me and was sorely disappointed when the first person out the door was Jack Drake rather than Olive. Olive stepped out right after and had a Huck treat ready on her palm. He snatched the cookie and wandered off to a nice sunny spot in her yard to enjoy his snack.

Olive had a hard time leaving her house. The impediment was more mental than physical. She just didn't feel comfortable leaving the cozy confines of her home. That was why I always arrived with a basket of food, and Jack quite often did the same with food from his restaurant. Jack Drake was normally all smiles. He was always pleasant and charming, but this morning, he looked distraught.

"Morning, Anna," he said with little energy.

"Jack, is everything all right?"

"Our poor Jack is being bullied by that horrid pastry chef and his overpriced bakery," Olive answered for him.

"It's still happening?" I asked, lamely. "Of course it is. I'm so sorry, Jack." I thought about the dramatic scene that had played out this morning, but I decided not to mention it. I hated spreading gossip. And it was Jamie's private business. Besides, it wouldn't help Jack in any way.

"He claims he has a good friend who is a health inspector across the harbor, and he's going to ask his friend what can be done about the awful smells coming from my restaurant."

"Awful smells?" I asked.

"Those were his exact words." Jack looked so hurt by it all, it was almost hard to recognize him, stooped and frowning as he was.

"There must be something that can be done," I said.

"Yes, have the man pack up his bags of flour and convection ovens and move back to the mainland," he said with a tight jaw. "But that's not going to happen. Anyhow, it's not your worry." He forced a smile and looked at my basket. "I'll bet your goodies will outshine the cold fried chicken and chocolate cake I just delivered to Olive. All my desserts were left untouched yesterday. People were heading to the bakery after their meal."

"I think everyone will tire of his baked goods soon enough. And they're so expensive. Besides, his brownies are subpar."

Jack's face popped up. He squinted at me. "Ah ha, so my good friend, Anna, is buying brownies from my enemy."

I felt a light blush warm my wind chapped cheeks. "Guess I let that secret out of the bag, but, in my defense, I just wanted to know what all the fuss was about. I have to say the brownie was nothing special. Mine are much better." There was no need to bring up the fabulous loaf of sourdough.

"Well, I've got to get back and start chopping vegetables. If you want more chocolate cake, Olive, just send a text, and I'll have someone deliver it straight away."

Olive pulled her sweater closer around her shoulders. "Thank you, Jack, and try not to worry about it too much. I hate to see you so upset."

Jack waved weakly and headed out of the yard.

Olive's look of concern vanished but then quickly returned when she saw her next bearer of goodies was not much happier than her last.

"Uh oh, you too? Come inside, the doctor is in." She stepped back from her doorway and waved me through.

Johnny, Olive's rock and roll crooning scarlet macaw, was standing on the back of the couch. His bright red head bobbed up and down when he saw me. "Awk! Anna baby!" It was my own personal greeting that he'd started a few months back, and I was thrilled about it.

Olive shuffled past me. "I'll put on a pot of tea and then you can tell me why the long face."

I followed Olive into her tiny kitchen and set the basket on the counter. "I've brought potato hash from breakfast and some of those sweet potato biscuits. Would you like me to heat some now?"

"Not now. I had two pieces of toast with marmalade this morning. Couldn't eat another bite, but those goodies will make a nice lunch."

I lifted the jar of honey butter out of the basket and set it to the side with the plate of biscuits. Olive opened the foil on the hash and took a deep whiff. "Hmm, can't wait." She placed the dish in her refrigerator. "My friends are all too good to me. Now, I couldn't do or say much to make Jack feel any better, but I'm sure I can help my friend Anna. Have a seat and I'll get the tea."

The smell of cinnamon filled the air as Olive filled two teacups with hot water. Johnny had joined us in the kitchen. His massive wings fluttered enough to send a napkin across the table. He landed gracefully on the top of Olive's favorite chair. His long tail swung gently to and fro allowing him to balance on his new perch.

Olive walked over with the two cups and placed one in front of me before sitting down. She lifted the cup for Johnny to smell the tea. He bobbed his head up and down with approval.

I laughed. "I agree, Johnny. There's nothing like cinnamon to brighten a mood." I took a cautious sip of the hot tea and set it down, leaving my hands to warm up on the porcelain cup.

"What's got you so down, Anna?" Olive asked after a cautious blow on her tea.

"I don't know if it's down or just uneasy. The house is filled with guests, two to be precise, but two that have had enough impact on the general state of the place that it feels as if six new people have arrived."

Olive sat forward with interest. "Goodness, who are these guests?"

"One is my mother." That revelation caused her to sit back somewhat disappointed.

"I now understand that little frown you're wearing. Your mother has only come to Frostfall a few times and every visit sours your mood."

"Is that terrible?" I picked up the tea for another sip. "I mean, I should be excited to see her, but I think she's only here to try and talk Cora into moving back to the city. It's come to her attention, apparently, that there are no fragile, ancient billionaires scooting around the island behind their walkers."

"It's not terrible at all. Whenever my mother, God rest her soul, and I used to meet up for a visit, all I could think about was pulling out a bottle of whiskey to numb myself from her presence. I loved her, but we just never saw eye to eye on anything. I was her only daughter with three brothers. So she was laser focused on every step I made growing up. She kept tabs on my friends and just about put any boy who'd dare ask me out through an FBI background check."

I could always count on Olive to make me smile. "It's funny you brought up the FBI because that brings me to another reason for this." I ran my hand around my face to remind her of the frown issue.

Olive pushed her long braid off her shoulder and sat forward with interest again. Her solitude and close to hermit existence made her an extra good listener. She was always anxious to hear interesting news. "Have the FBI been involved in something on the island? I sensed that something was up. The island always vibrates with energy when things have gone astray. Was it a murder? Have they finally decided that ridiculous Detective Norwich can't do the job properly, so they sent the big guns?"

I almost hated to tell her the truth. It would be such a letdown from the scenario she'd just conjured.

"None of those things. Although, I can only hope that someday the higherups will decide that Detective Norwich should be demoted to parking ticket duty. This has to do with Nate." I spoke up quickly before she could run off with another exciting narrative. "His friend is here for a short visit. He's the one who will be joining the FBI. Arlo used to work with Nate on the force, and I think—no—I know Nate is jealous about his friend's move up the career ladder."

Olive put on that empathic smile that I would've, just once, liked to see on my mom, the person whose ear I should have had for these kinds of troubles, but that had never been the case. "Anna, you're worried Nate will get antsy here on this island and leave you."

My throat tightened at the whole notion being said out loud. I took a deep breath. "I'm mad for letting myself get so attached. I was having a perfectly good life of independence. After the heartbreak with Michael, I'd found my rhythm. I was my own person. And now, I've become that silly, self-conscious teenager waiting for the darn phone to ring." Bringing up Michael had reminded me of the shocking discovery I'd made about an uninvited guest at our small wedding, but I decided that was one story too much for this morning. Besides, it was in the past, and I didn't know what to even make of it. I lay in my dark room for an hour fretting about it until I reminded myself that none of it mattered because Michael was gone.

"Nonsense, you're not silly. It's a legitimate concern. You've invested time, energy and a slice of your heart into this relationship with Nate, and you have every right to know where you stand. Why don't you bring this concern up to him?"

"I don't want to look like that silly teen. I want Nate to know I'm independent and that his decisions are his to make... even if they'll break my heart. Honestly, Olive, if he's starting to feel that claustrophobia people get when living on an island, there's not much I'll be able to say or do to change that. He had a career in law enforcement. He says he enjoys working on the construction crew, but is it enough to keep him here? This visit from his friend makes me think no. He needs more than hammering on a lighthouse and walking home to a boarding house filled with eccentric housemates."

Olive's smile was always comforting. She reached across her small table. The uneven legs caused a slight wobble, but the tea remained in the cups. Her hands were always dry from painting. "Whatever happens, Anna, just remember you've got a lot of friends on this island who love you."

I placed my hand over hers. "Thank you, Olive. I knew our visit would help me cheer up."

fourteen

THE CHAT with Olive had given me a somewhat new outlook on life. My mom's visit would end soon. She never liked to stay long on the island, or at the boarding house, for that matter. Something told me her entire master plan to lure Cora back to the city had been undermined by the arrival of Nate's friend. Cora hardly had time for Mom. Whether she stayed or not, I decided not to let her mom-ness get to me anymore. My renewed energy and lifted spirits prompted me to plan for some luscious lemon bars to serve at movie night. The one flaw in my plan was that I didn't have any lemons, and they were a necessity for lemon bars.

I dropped a worn out dog at the house. It was still quiet upstairs except for the sounds coming from Opal's television —a Katherine Hepburn movie from the sound of it. It was hard to mistake that voice. Mom had said she was tired, and she wanted to read her book. I knew her glumness stemmed from lack of progress on the Cora front. I tiptoed around the kitchen not wanting to alert her to my presence. I was still rejuvenating my mood, and I didn't need her to come downstairs and dampen it again.

The sun was getting warmer and brighter, so I pulled on one of my straw hats and set out toward Molly's produce stand. Each new day in spring brought more life to the island. Others might have found Frostfall too small and claustrophobic, but I saw a different scene every time I stepped outside. I spotted a curious buckeye, one of the first of the season, was checking out some of the early yarrow. Its big spots resembled giant eyeballs, a trick of nature that scared possible predators into believing a large animal with big eyes was staring back at them. This little winged visitor was the harbinger of things to come. Before long, bright orange monarchs, neon yellow sulphurs and energetic coppers would be dancing in and out of the wildflowers.

My steps felt much lighter than earlier when I'd carried the weight of the world on my shoulders to Olive's house. I was determined to stay positive and constantly remind myself of the wonderful life I had on Frostfall Island. Tonight was movie night, a big night at the boarding house, and I planned to focus all of my attention on making it a perfect evening.

Molly's produce stand looked nearly depleted of its usual rainbow of fruits and vegetables, but her lemon basket was still full. Sera was at the stand, but she wasn't holding her usual shopping basket. Both women looked up from their conversation as my shoes padded along the boardwalk.

"Anna, you're back for a second round?" Molly motioned to the canvas bag I had under my arm.

"Just need some lemons."

Sera sighed loudly to let me know she was upset. I hardly needed the sound effects. Her face showed it all.

"Another slow morning?" I asked, hesitantly.

"Yes. I've got your sister doing some much needed spring cleaning. I don't think she's too happy about it. I doubt too many people wear diamond watches while they're wiping down tables and stockroom shelves. I was just telling Molly, I've got enough reserve for another month of terrible business, then I have to start thinking of moving on."

Her words made me gasp. "Moving on? You mean off the island?"

She shrugged. "Naturally, it's the last thing I want. Samuel too. Although, he has far less attachment to Frostfall. But if I can't make a living, then I can't stay. It's as simple as that."

It felt like someone had hit me in the gut. It was one blow after another this week, and I wondered when it would stop.

"Just hang in there, Sera," I said. "My intuition tells me things are going to work out. Don't make any hasty decisions."

"I hope you're right, Anna. I'd hate to leave this place. All my friends are here." A much needed three way hug helped bring back smiles all around.

As we parted, we all took note of Murray Hogan walking, in fact, marching, along the boardwalk. Murray Hogan was married to Sally Hogan, the overworked bakery assistant. He was a big man in his late fifties, who walked with a slight hunch due to a back injury he sustained on a fishing boat. He had thick pock marked skin from a bad bout of chicken pox as a child. Everything about him seemed rough and salty, like an old sea dog, but you could always count on him to be cheerful. Not today. His fists were clenched. His jaw was even tighter, and his hunch was more pronounced as he lumbered angrily toward the harbor. He was coming from the direction of the bakery.

"Everything all right, Murray?" Molly called, but he ignored us and muttered something under his breath as he stormed past. We all stared in silent shock as Murray continued down the boardwalk, presumably toward home.

"I don't think I've ever seen Murray Hogan in that kind of mood," Molly said.

"That was strange," I agreed. I knew a little more than I was letting on, but again, I didn't want to start a big rumor. My intuition was telling me Murray's angry march had to do with the new baker. It seemed Quentin was causing a lot of people to curl their fists and let their tempers get the best of them.

"I'm going to head back to the tea shop and pout," Sera said. "I've got a tray of tomato tarts in the oven if anyone's interested." Sera headed off toward the 3Ts.

"Poor thing," Molly said. "I'm really worried about her. If the bakery continues to pull away all her customers, she'll have to shut down the tea shop."

"Let's hope it doesn't come to that, Molly."

Abner Plunkett, the sixty something, fast moving man who ran the Frostfall Historical Society and Maritime Museum strolled up to the produce stand. "Did you save those two apples for me, Molly?"

Molly ducked behind her stand. "Sure did, Abner. Picked the two prettiest apples." Molly's own apple cheeks rounded as she held out each piece of fruit on her palms.

"Those are perfect, Molly, thanks." Abner smiled at me. "Anna, I didn't see you there hunched over the lemon basket. Let me guess. Lemon Bundt cake?"

"Lemon bars but now you've got me rethinking my whole lemon plan."

Abner had one of those gentle laughs that often ended with a quiet snort. Today was no different.

"Abner," Molly started as she counted out his change. "Did you happen to see Murray Hogan before you walked over here?"

Abner had light fuzz on the top of his head. It was a silvery gray with the occasional patch of brown. He glanced toward the museum end of the boardwalk and moved closer with a little lift of his shoulders as if he had something quite important to discuss. "I sure did see him." Abner held an apple in each hand as he narrated the events. "Murray showed up at the bakery this morning. I just happened to be outside the museum setting up the sign for the day. By the way, we're starting our annual buy two museum tickets get one free sale. You girls should drop by and get yours before we run out. So, I'm out on the boardwalk setting up my sign when I see Murray Hogan storm past the long line of bakery customers." Abner rolled his eyes. "People are going to regret eating all those baked goods." He lifted a hand with a shiny red blushed apple. "This is all the dessert I need. I don't have any intention of leaving this earth early just because I couldn't turn down a chocolate croissant."

I'd forgotten how chatty Abner could be, especially after a long dreary winter when he was stuck in his cold, drafty museum dusting off the town's beloved pirate displays and waiting for a visitor or two to step through the door.

"But why was Murray so angry?" Molly prodded.

"I can't tell you for sure, but I think it has to do with his wife, Sally. She was so excited to get the bakery job, but I think she's feeling nothing but regret now. That Oxley is a hard boss. I've seen Sally walk out in tears. He works her hard. With those long lines, he needs at least three people behind the counter. It's far too much for one person. My theory is that he likes that long line because it makes people notice his bakery, and since everyone seems willing to spend an hour waiting for one of his breads or pastries, he probably doesn't feel the need to hire anyone else. But I'm sure poor Sally will be at a breaking point soon."

"Murray certainly seemed to be at his," I noted.

"Indeed." Abner nodded energetically. "The two men had heated words right outside the bakery before Oxley threatened to fire Sally if Murray didn't leave. That was all I saw before the phone rang in the museum, and I had to race in to answer it. Thanks for picking out these apples, Molly. Can't wait to eat them." Abner was one of those wiry, thin people who rarely stood still. His feet practically flew over the boardwalk as he hurried back to the museum.

"I don't think anyone has ever moved to this island and caused as much disruption and chaos as Quentin Oxley," Molly said.

"I agree, Molly, and maybe it's time someone talks to him about it."

fifteen

I HAD no idea why I decided to take it upon myself to be the town speaker. It might have been that my mom had made me feel ornery and on defense, or maybe, I just wanted to keep the peace because that meant no trouble and that meant a murder free spring for Anna, the impromptu detective.

Apparently, Quentin had not stopped his morning hurricane of anger with Jack, Jamie and Murray. Remi Seymour was walking briskly out of the bakery as I passed by Jack's restaurant. Tears ran down her face as she stared down at her sandals. She hurried past and headed to her bicycle. It took her several tries to line the numbers up on her bike lock. She kept swiping at the tears as she spun the tiny numbers around in their chamber. I was just seconds from walking over to help her when the lock opened. She climbed on the bike and pedaled off, still whisking away tears as she went.

I was now even more energized to talk to our newest citizen. I'd seen six people who were normally happy, pleasant locals, either yelling, waving fists, crying or fretting about their business. This had to end. I let the ten people in line know that I wasn't cutting ahead to buy anything, that I just needed to talk to the owner. No one had any objections, so I continued to the door. Sally was dashing back and forth behind the counter, placing delicate pastries and cookies into pink boxes with the care and skill of a surgeon. It seemed she wasn't willing to put up with another humiliating lecture about handling the baked goods too clumsily. Of course, the extra care she was taking meant that each order took much longer. There was no sign of Quentin. As much as I hated to interrupt Sally's flow, I needed to find the man responsible for putting half the island on edge.

I managed to make my way up to the counter where Sally was cautiously piling petit fours into a box. "Sally, I hate to bother you, but where's your boss?"

Sally glanced up for a split second. "I'd like to know that myself. Some man came into the shop about five minutes ago, and they both walked out. He left me here all alone."

"I'm sorry about that, Sally." I headed back out and looked around. Two deep voices floated up from the narrow alley between the bakery and the museum. I neared the edge of the bakery building and peered around the corner. It wasn't the least bit surprising to find Oxley in yet another heated argument. What was shocking was that I didn't recognize his opponent. At least, I was sure he wasn't a local. Something about the way the man stood, shoulders slightly forward and head jutting out far on his neck, looked familiar. Was he the man I saw standing in the shadows this morning? I would have bet a tray of my best brownies on it.

"I've told you I do not have your sourdough starter. I've made my own starter, and frankly, it's much better than that ancient old batch your family's been using. Now, I have a business to run. I suggest you get off the island. If you continue to follow and harass me, I'll call the police." Any local would have laughed at that meaningless threat, but someone who didn't know the island might take it to heart. Even so, the man still looked plenty mad, and there was another pair of fists for me to add to my list of tight fists.

I stepped back when the man stomped off. I'd seen more than my share of stomping and marching too. Before Quentin could slip into the side door to the kitchen, I turned the corner.

"Mr. Oxley, I need a word."

I was sure I detected an eye roll. He was quickly becoming as disliked as Norwich on my people to dislike list. "I'm busy."

"I don't care. We need to talk."

He lowered his hand from the door and crossed his arms to let me know just how annoyed he was with my interruption.

I met his arm cross with one of my own, only mine was showing outrage. "My name is Anna St. James. I'm a longtime resident on this island, and I don't usually need to say this to new citizens but in your case, I'll make an exception. We take pride on being a friendly, help each other in times of need kind of community."

"Isn't that quaint," he said with another eye roll.

"It's not quaint. It's part of a concept I like to call human decency. Something you seem to lack."

"You don't even know me."

"Oh, but I do, and not through any personal interaction with you—until now—and trust me, it'll be our last. You have at least half a dozen normally content people upset and angry."

His mouth tilted wickedly. "You're talking about that joke of a fisherman. Maybe if he didn't smell like dead fish his girlfriend wouldn't have come running to me."

"This is a small island, and trouble never goes unnoticed. That man, just now, he's not a local. I've seen him lurking around your bakery. That tells me you're not only upsetting locals, but your troublemaking is spilling onto our shores from across the harbor."

Quentin still had his arms crossed but he shrugged. "No trouble. He came here to accuse me of stealing his family's sourdough starter."

"And did you?" I asked, plainly. Molly had mentioned that Quentin claimed to have a hundred-year-old sourdough starter, a family treasure of sorts. Was he talking about a family he didn't actually belong to?

He didn't respond, which was all I needed to *not* hear. "I need to get back to my shop. If you're through with your school teacher lecture, I've got more important things to do than listen to some old spinster." He looked pointedly at my ringless finger. "Go sip tea with the other old crows and leave me alone."

"What? You mean you're not going to call the police on me? I've heard you say that more than once." Admittedly, I probably shouldn't have divulged that, but he had my temper on fire.

He squinted down at me through dropped lids. "Are you spying on me? Maybe I should call the police."

"Yes, I think you should. Oh, by the way, there is no law enforcement on this island. In fact, when there's trouble, there's one non-official person who gets called to the scene."

"Really? Who is this person, so I can get them on speed dial. I think I need to give them a call."

"Don't bother. You can't have my number. If you need help, maybe you can turn to your sourdough starter. Oh, and by the way, your brownies are inferior." I spun around and did my own little march and fist clench as I walked out of the alleyway.

sixteen

"WINSTON, put those last three chairs right here." I glanced up toward the portable screen. "I think this will be the best spot." Winston had come home early to help set up for movie night. His new girlfriend, Alyssa, was joining us this evening, and he was more than a little nervous about it. I told him we'd all try our hardest not to embarrass him. However, I was making no promises about old timer chitchat because we Gen X and Boomers liked to reminisce. Unfortunately, Sera and Sam just weren't in the mood to join us.

It had taken me a few hours to cool my head after the unfortunate chat with Oxley. At least I could now sympathize more readily with all the people he was hurting. My intuition told me somewhere, somehow, something was going to have to give. Quentin's presence on our small island was like a volcano building up pressure just waiting to erupt.

Mom and Opal had sat at the table sipping tea and chatting while I made the lemon bars. My mom could be quite charming and fun to talk to in a casual conversation, as long as you weren't her daughter. Opal and Mom were close in age and had plenty to talk about. Cora dragged in about halfway through my baking session. She'd left the house with a neatly clipped bun but returned with most of her hair hanging in sad thick fringes around her face. Mom immediately fretted that she was working her fingers to the bone and all for a pittance.

Cora agreed but then with plenty of energy hurried up the stairs to get ready for movie night. I wasn't kidding myself. She wasn't as excited about our slightly hokey outdoor movie event as she was about sitting next to Arlo. Cora never thought ahead. She was growing quite attached to her new acquaintance, but he would be leaving before she really got to know him. I hoped she wasn't setting herself up for a big downfall... like her sister.

"Anna, should I start the popcorn?" Toby asked. We'd collected money as a household to purchase the various items needed for an outdoor theater. Besides the large retractable screen and projector, we bought beanbag chairs, a popcorn maker and a significant supply of movie theater type candy. The beanbags, we'd decided, stacked nicely in the storage shed, and they were easy to clean. Fortunately, our theater capacity had expanded with the addition of four extra beanbags after Tobias spotted a sale online. I was sure Cora would have rather just shared a beanbag with Arlo, but I wasn't in the mood to watch my mom's head explode. I'd had a stressful enough day as it was.

Normally, when something had upset me, I would talk to

Nate about it, but he'd been out all day with his friend. They trudged in as we were pulling out the beanbags. Nate put the bicycles away while Arlo lent a hand with the bags.

Arlo and Winston pulled out the last two beanbags as Tobias fired up the popcorn machine. Arlo took a deep whiff of the cool evening air. "Is there any smell more familiar or nostalgic than popcorn?" Arlo rubbed his hands together. "What are we watching? I heard that last Tom Cruise action flick is terrific." Nate returned just as he finished the comment.

"Sorry, mate, we watch movie classics. They lend themselves better to the whole ambience of an under the stars theater." Nate had always liked our movie night extravaganzas, corny as they were.

Arlo didn't seem as enamored. "You mean to tell me we're going to sit out here in the cold and watch old timey black and white movies?"

"Yup," I said curtly and headed toward the house. I hadn't meant to snap at him, and I was just about to turn around and apologize when Cora splashed out of the house in a glittering silver dress and matching shoes, a practical outfit for beanbags. The only thing missing was the diamond tiara. My short reply was quickly forgotten when the dazzle that was Cora Cromwell entered the scene. Even Winston and Tobias, who had both seen Cora at her fanciest, stopped what they were doing to watch my silver plated sister descend the back steps. Arlo let out a loud whistle. Huck dashed out of the house, assuming it was for him.

I was off the hook for the apology, which suited my mood

just fine. I went into the kitchen. Mom was standing looking out the window. "Why on earth is your sister dressed for a night at the opera?"

I stopped and looked at her. "Seriously? Mom, Cora wears satin gloves to brush her teeth. Why wouldn't she wear silver sequins to a movie?"

"Oh, you exaggerate," Mom said. "She's just trying to impress that man out there. Arvin or Arty or whatever his name is."

"You know very well his name is Arlo, and yes, she's having fun flirting with the man. She doesn't meet many new men on the island." As I said it, I wanted to take my foot and kick myself on the bottom.

"See, then you agree. Cora's limiting her social life drastically on this island. Why don't you tell her that."

"Nope, not going to do it. Cora can leave when she wants. I'm not keeping her here. The truth is I think she's found enough friends and family here that she's enjoying it too much to leave."

My mom sighed the biggest most dejected sound I'd ever heard. "I'm going to go upstairs and put on a few more layers. It's much colder here than at home."

I set to work cutting the lemon bars. They'd turned out beautifully. The back door opened and Nate walked in. His longish hair was sticking out here and there. His disheveled appearance made me smile. He was one of those men who could pull off messy and rumpled as well as slick and spiffy.

"Did you two have fun today?" I asked.

"We did. We rode around the island, then took a long

swim. I forgot how much energy Arlo had. He's going to be great as a special agent."

"Special agent?" I asked. "Is that what his position is labeled?"

"He'll have to work his way up to that, but I have no doubt he'll get there." Nate came up behind me, put his arm gently around my waist and pressed his chest against my back. He smelled fresh and green from a day outside. His warm breath tickled the back of my neck. "Those lemon bars look amazing. And so do you." He kissed the side of my neck causing to me to break the lemon bar I was holding. Powdered sugar showered the plate and lemon curd coated my thumb.

"Oops, sorry about that." He dropped his arm and turned to lean against the counter and face me. "You seem distracted, Anna."

I blushed. "That was entirely your fault."

"I don't mean *that*. I mean in general. Arlo won't be here much longer. I know he's a lot." He glanced out the kitchen window to the scene outside. Cora was talking animatedly to Arlo, long pink fingernails waving in the air and her head dropping back with flirty laughter. "Your sister seems to like him." He paused. "Can't say the same for you."

My face popped up from my task. "What? Of course I do. He's quite the charmer. I like him very much." I had no intention of looking like a pathetic, lovesick woman by mentioning my worry that Arlo's visit might cause Nate to rethink his time here on the island. "I'm distracted because some of my good friends and some very good local people are being—well—terrorized—for lack of a better word, and, I'm sure there is one, but that's the one sticking in my brain right now."

My use of a word that was perhaps a bit too hyperbolic for the situation caused Nate to straighten. "Terrorized? What do you mean?"

"Again, that wasn't the best word. The new owner of the French bakery has been wreaking all manner of havoc on the island."

He relaxed. I'd caught him on more than one occasion turning on that adrenaline that probably helped him in his previous job. "Really? I've heard a lot of people talking about him but mostly about his baked goods. What's the problem?"

I shook my head not wanting to get into all the details. "First of all, his bakery has basically stolen all of Sera's customers. She's so distraught she's actually toying with the idea of leaving the island."

Nate nodded and picked up a crumb of the broken lemon bar. "Samuel did mention something to me about their business being really slow because everyone was at the bakery." He pushed the crumb into his mouth. "Hmm, whatever that guy is making, I'm sure none of it tastes as good as this."

"I did sample a brownie that didn't hold a candle to mine."

"Then Sera doesn't need to worry. Eventually, people will get tired of the bakery. It's just because it's new, and let's face it, not a lot of new things happen on this island." It was the second disparaging thing I'd heard him say about Frostfall Island since Arlo's arrival.

"I like the consistency of life here," I said, defensively.

"No complaints either," he added quickly.

"And then there's Jack Drake."

Nate stood up straighter again. He tended to be a little jealous about my friendship with Jack, which was silly because it was purely a friendship. (I didn't mind the jealousy thing either.) "What about Jack?" His dark brows were tucked together tensely. I had to tamp down a smile.

"Apparently, Quentin Oxley, the baker, has been threatening Jack with the health department. Oxley has some inside connection there, it seems."

"That's never good, the owner of a food establishment having connections with health inspectors." Nate picked up another crumb and ate it.

"Definitely a conflict. And there's no problem with Jack's restaurant. He's always kept a pretty tight ship. No pun intended. Oxley keeps complaining that the aromas from Jack's kitchen are drifting into his bakery and ruining his baked goods."

"Sounds like Oxley should have thought of that before he opened a bakery downwind from a seafood restaurant."

"I agree. This is his problem, but he's being relentless and Jack is distraught."

Opal entered the kitchen in almost as stunning a fashion as my sister with her fiery red hair and floral printed flowing house dress. "Those lemon bars smell divine," she said dramatically as if auditioning for a part on an old Greta Garbo movie. Opal always got into her old time movie actor persona on movie night. "Hurry, you two. Enough canoodling. Dracula awaits." She floated out of the house with long, dramatic steps.

Nate looked at me. "Dracula?"

"It's Bela Lugosi night," I reminded him.

He nodded approvingly. "Cool."

seventeen

HALFWAY THROUGH *DRACULA* my mom excused herself saying she was too tired and cold to stick out a double feature, but I knew it was because Cora and Arlo had subtly moved their beanbags into a more shadowy part of the yard for a little, as Opal phrased it, canoodling. It was too much for Mom to handle. We had to put the movie on pause to hoist my mom from the beanbag chair. She also commented that it was certainly going to be her last time sitting in a beanbag chair. That was probably for the best.

Alyssa and Winston were having their own little hand holding time. They'd scooted their two chairs closer and had a bucket of popcorn between them. Alyssa was a petite, quiet little thing with big brown eyes peering out from under a fringe of long bangs. It was hard to picture her handling scared and sometimes dangerous wildlife, but Winston had said more than once that she was a natural, a true Dr. Dolittle.

Opal and Tobias had been sharing a bucket of popcorn as well. They seemed to be enjoying the movie as they reminisced about going to the movies as kids. Back then double features were expected and candy and popcorn could be bought with a song and a dance. Not literally, of course, but it was certainly more affordable. Not like today when there was just one movie and the treats were so expensive you had to sneak in your own goodies.

Nate and I were having our own date night holding hands between the beanbags. My mom was still utterly clueless that Nate and I were a couple. That had to do either with the fact that we were pretty good at concealing our feelings for each other, or the fact that my mom had little interest in my personal relationships unless they somehow affected Cora. In this case, my personal relationship sort of did affect my sister. She was absolutely smitten with Arlo. My sister always had a lot of relationships, but it was rare for her to be smitten. The smitten-ness always came from the other direction. I hoped she wouldn't be too upset when Arlo packed up and left.

Bela Lugosi took his final bite just as an ornery breeze kicked up. Opal laughed as their popcorn bucket and its contents were picked up by the wind. Popcorn sprayed everywhere.

"The birds are going to be very happy in the morning," Winston said as he hopped up (one of the few of us who could hop out of a beanbag) to retrieve the popcorn bucket. He'd just retrieved that one when Cora's bucket flew off on a gust.

Winston looked at me. "I don't think that screen can outlast a spring wind. Should we call it a night?"

"But I was waiting for Doris Day," Opal said. "I planned it so that her cheerful beauty would wash away the dark, kind of creepy feeling left behind by Bela Lugosi." As she explained her movie choices, a particularly sharp, strong burst of wind slapped all of us with cold air.

Opal sat forward. "Never mind, Doris. That wind is cold. Guess we'll save it for next movie night."

We moved faster as the wind picked up even more. "Nice thing about beanbags," Nate noted as he helped me carry some to the storage shed, "is that they are literally the paper-weights of the chair world."

We had a good laugh as we stepped into the dark shed. I reached around for the light switch, but Nate took my hand and pulled me to him. "Not so fast with the light switch, St. James." He kissed me. Before letting me go, he gazed deeply into my eyes. "What else is bothering you, Anna? And don't go on a rant about that baker."

I still didn't have the fortitude to tell him my deepest worry, that he'd be leaving the island soon. "It really does have mostly to do with that horrid man. I guess I left out a big chunk when I failed to mention that I had a slight confrontation with Oxley myself."

There it went again, the adrenaline induced posture. "A confrontation?" Nate asked, urgently. "What do you mean? Did he touch you? What happened?" The questions were shooting out like bullets from an automatic weapon.

"No, he didn't touch me." I patted Nate's chest. "I started

the confrontation, so anything that transpired was my fault. I simply told him he was stirring up too much controversy and causing a lot of trouble for an island where we pride ourselves on the lack of trouble."

My calm explanation seemed to help. His stance loosened some. "Aside from the more than occasional murder," he reminded me.

"You've been listening to Opal too much. Anyhow, I can safely say that Quentin Oxley might make a fabulous loaf of sourdough, but he is not a good neighbor and not a credit to the community. He was rude, almost offensive in his manner. But I let him know where I stood."

Nate was shaking his head before I finished. "Anna, sometimes you take on too much to keep this island running smoothly. You're already the go-to person for crimes and murder. Let someone else work on community outreach."

I smiled. "I don't think our contentious chat today could have been categorized as community outreach."

"You know what I mean. Let Drake deal with his abrasive neighbor. The bakery doesn't affect you."

"But this place is my home, Nate." I tried to hide my disappointment at his comment, but he noticed.

"You know what I mean." He kissed my forehead. "I just worry about you. So what else? You said 'mostly'."

"I don't understand."

"You said it had mostly to do with the horrid baker. What's the other part of the mostly?"

A gust blew against the shed, shaking it on its foundation. It startled me into Nate's arms for a second. "Guess I better get the flashlights ready," I said. "Could be quite the storm."

"I agree and I would also like to point out that you're avoiding my question."

I decided then it was time to confess. "It's just I'm worried that seeing Arlo might make you—you know—the big city, special agent, FBI, all that stuff is putting stars in your eyes."

His mouth tilted in wry grin. "Were those stars that obvious?"

"The only thing shinier is Cora's silver dress."

Nate laughed. I was glad the moment had gone that direction, lighter rather than more serious. I wasn't ready for that kind of talk after the day I had.

"I just want you to be happy," I said. "I support you no matter what your decision.

"My decision? Anna, I promise you it hasn't gone past the stars in my eyes stage yet. I enjoy my life here on the island, working at the lighthouse, spending time with the people in our, as you put it, Moon River family and most of all, I love coming down to breakfast every morning and seeing your beautiful face. If I did ever decide to go back into law enforcement, and yes, occasionally, I think about it, then that wouldn't mean things between us would end. After all, there's a ferry and only a short harbor to cross. It would be a long distance relationship."

I forced a smile. I'd known people who tried hard to keep a relationship going with someone across the harbor. It was true the distance wasn't that great, but that stretch of miles was filled with Atlantic Ocean. It wasn't like hopping in your car and driving a few miles on the highway. The harbor crossing was an obstacle.

"You're right, Nate. I'm worrying about nothing," I said quietly. "We better finish cleaning up before those gale force winds start kicking the island around."

eighteen

I RETURNED from my pre-dawn art session to quite the scene. Cora was standing on the front steps, teary eyed and waving her handkerchief as Arlo, backpack on shoulder, blew her kisses. It was like a World War II movie where the wife watched as her soldier walked off into the sunset, only it was sunrise and the soldier was off to the Federal Bureau of Investigations instead of war. Nate stood nearby, waiting to walk his friend to the harbor. It seemed as if he was trying hard not to be amused by the theatrics. I hated to admit that I felt more than a little relief after Arlo announced that he'd been called to start his new position a few days early and that he'd be leaving Frostfall in the morning. I just hadn't realized how early. He wanted to catch the first ferry out, so he had no choice except to start off at the crack of dawn. His announcement had brought a great deal of sad moans from my sister. My mom, on the other hand, had practically danced off to bed for the night.

Cora waited until she could no longer see the men before turning around with a final wipe of her eyes and heading inside. Huck and I circled around and went in through the kitchen. No one else was downstairs yet. Cora went straight upstairs to shower.

I got to work on a batch of biscuits to go with some scrambled eggs. Winston was the first to come downstairs. "Can't stay for breakfast, Anna," he said as he poured himself some coffee.

"Let me guess. Chocolate croissants?"

He put the pot down. "No, Alyssa decided, as delicious as they are, they're far too fattening. I'm somewhat relieved. They're very expensive."

"Ah ha, that is my theory playing out in real time, and I thank you and Alyssa for being part of my experiment."

Winston stopped the cup halfway to his mouth. "Huh?"

"Nothing. Don't mind me. I'm babbling. Why are you skipping breakfast?"

"Two baby harbor seals are coming in this morning. I've got to get the enclosure cleaned up. Alyssa said she'd make me a breakfast sandwich."

"It's going well between you," I noted.

Winston's massive head of blond hair always made him look younger. "It's going really well. Thanks for the coffee." He drank the rest and put the empty cup in the sink. "See you at dinner." I watched as he hurried out the back door. I wondered if I'd be losing a tenant soon. Alyssa had a sweet little cottage near Calico Peak in the center of the island. Winston didn't take up nearly as much 'air space' as the other more eccentric people in the house, but it wouldn't be the same without him and his constant parade of rescue critters. I was getting ahead of myself. They'd only been dating a few months, like Nate and me. Was I getting ahead of myself there too? I grunted, frustrated with my own psyche for putting so much doubt into my thoughts. Then, as if on cue, my psyche, personified, strolled merrily into the kitchen. My mom was definitely a wear-it-all-on-your-sleeve type of person, and she was thrilled that Arlo had gone.

Naturally, she wanted to make sure of it before she took the cheeriness thing too far. She poured herself a cup of coffee. "I assume everyone got well on their way this morning."

"I don't know about everyone, but Arlo is gone. I guess that's the *everyone* you were talking about." Why was it—just ten seconds with my mom in the room and my defenses were up and ready to fight.

Mom scowled at me over her coffee cup to let me know she disapproved of the sarcasm. She sat at the table. "I, for one, thought Arlo was too loud, and he ate too much. He couldn't possibly expect you to keep feeding him at that rate."

"He didn't eat more than anyone else. You were just more focused on him because you worried he'd up and leave with your precious daughter."

Mom shrugged. She was wearing a silky shirt that shimmered under the kitchen lights. It was easy to see where my sister got her love for everything shiny and sumptuous. "I won't deny it. I'm glad to see him go. He wasn't right for

112

Cora. I just wish your sister would come back to the city where she can meet a good match."

"Yes, you've made that quite clear." I rolled out my biscuit dough and set to work cutting out the circles.

"Nate is much more likable," Mom said. "I noticed he looks at you a great deal. Maybe you should think about it. He seems like a sensible man, and he's very handsome."

I decided to ignore her remarks. "When do you think you might be leaving, Mom?"

"Why? Are you ready to get rid of me?"

"Not at all. It's just that you usually get antsy on this little island." Immediate guilt swept through me. Was I trying to get rid of her? I rarely saw Mom anymore, and here I was anxious to see her pack her stuff. I was a terrible daughter.

"That's true. I don't know how you two can stand this lumpy little chunk of land. It's like living in the middle—the middle—"

"Of an ocean?" I asked wryly. The moment of guilt had passed. "That's sort of the point of an island."

"Now you're just being ornery, and you know why that is?" she asked.

I wanted to answer with because my mother is visiting, but I was sure she had a much more cutting reason. "Gosh, no, Mom, what could it be?" I was still talking like a teenager on defense.

"Because you're lonely. You need a husband. Michael's been gone for nearly a decade. It's time to move on. I always told you your career in business was going to be a great opportunity to meet eligible men."

"And by eligible, you mean, wealthy."

She did a haughty little wriggle on her chair as she picked up her coffee. "There are worse things than being rich."

"Yes, but it's not required for happiness. I'm happy here, Mom. I wasn't happy in my career."

"How do you know? You were only out in the financial world a few years before Michael dragged you away to this island."

Before I could give my fiery response, a loud, frantic knock rattled the front door. "Anna! Anna, we need you!"

"Abner?" I muttered as I pulled off my apron and hurried to the front door.

Abner was breathing hard. His face was a mixture of creamy white and dark pink. "Anna, thank goodness you're home. You need to come. There's been a murder."

nineteen

ABNER WAS SO FAST on his light little legs, I had to run to keep pace with him. "It's just awful. I don't know what happened," he said between breaths. His phone rang in the pocket of the blue blazer he always wore at the museum. He fumbled with it a second before managing to get it to his ear. "Hello? Yes, we're coming. Yes, Anna is with me. We're just reaching the boardwalk. I can move faster if I'm not on the phone," he said curtly before shoving the phone back into his pocket.

We rounded the corner and turned toward the museum. I was still entirely in the dark about the victim, the location and the circumstances. For a fleeting, frightening moment, I worried something had happened to Jack. There was a large group of people huddled near the Pirate's Gold Restaurant.

"Abner," I said breathlessly, "it's not Jack is it?"

Abner stumbled slightly at the suggestion. "What? Heavens no. Why, I thought it'd be quite obvious." As we neared the scene, I realized what he meant. It was the bakery.

"Is it—?" I asked.

"Yes, and as shocked as I am, I'm not surprised." Abner elbowed his way through the onlookers. Mutterings about the horrible scene inside the bakery rumbled around the crowd.

"Where's Sally?" I asked as I scanned the faces.

"Someone said she was fired yesterday. Customers were lined up this morning, as usual, and when it was time to open Irene Vella knocked on the door. She expected to see Sally. That was when someone at the back of the line yelled that Sally had been fired yesterday after a big argument with Quentin. Irene waited a few minutes before giving the door a push. It was locked. I happened to step outside of the museum to sweep the boardwalk—someone tracked a lot of sand into the museum yesterday." Abner shook his head. It always seemed slightly oversized for his body. "Not important. But I decided to find out what was going on. There was no answer on the front door, so I went around to the side door. That was the door Quentin used the most." The side door to the bakery reminded me of my own unpleasant conversation with Oxley. Abner took a deep breath. "I walked in through the side door." His voice cracked, and he patted his chest. "It's hard to think about. I saw the body and rushed out through this front door. I was afraid I'd already disturbed evidence at the side entrance. I instructed everyone to stay outside the bakery unless they wanted to witness something horrific and at the same time be implicated in a murder. Then I took off running to get you."

"I'm sorry you experienced all this, Abner. I better get inside. I'll need to confirm things before I call Detective Norwich to the island." The name caused Abner to roll his eyes. Everyone on Frostfall knew that Norwich was a nitwit. It was why they always called me rather than him, but the officials needed to be notified. Unfortunately for the island, our designated *official* was none other than Detective Buckston Norwich, a sloppy, rude man who couldn't solve a crime even if it happened directly in front of him and the murderer confessed.

"I think confirmation will be quick and easy." Abner reached for the door and stopped just short of opening it. Most of the color added by the brisk walk to the bakery had washed away. "I'm sorry, Anna. I went in there for a second —" He swallowed hard. "I just can't." He looked down in shame.

I patted his arm. "It's all right, Abner. I understand completely." The bitter smell of smoke hit me the second I stepped inside the bakery. Dark streams of it curled up from beneath the door to the kitchen. My eyes and throat burned. My heart raced. Was the place on fire? The front of the shop looked completely normal, stacks of fluffy pastries and chewy cookies waiting to be placed into boxes and bags. Everything I knew about firefighting I'd learned from television. That information felt comically inadequate now, but I was sure firemen always touched a door first to make sure huge flames weren't lapping at the other side of the door just waiting for that burst of oxygen from the next room. I touched the door to the kitchen. It was warm but not hot. I took a bigger whiff and coughed at the smoke that came with it, the sugar filled smoke. I'd smelled the same odor whenever I burned a cake in the oven.

I held my breath, both to avoid smoke inhalation and to brace myself for what I was about to see. Abner's fear assured me it wasn't going to be pretty. The kitchen was filled with smoke. As I'd guessed, it was coming from the ovens. I waved my hands unable to see much in the small room except the silver glint of the work table. There were mounds of dough, stretched and folded and waiting to be proofed. I hurried to the ovens and shut them off. Whatever was inside, charring to a crisp, would have to wait. I smacked the button for the kitchen exhaust. It started up with a loud rumble and slowly began sipping away the smoke. My eyes were clouded with burning tears as I made my way around the large stainless steel work table. My toe tapped something on the floor. I froze and looked slowly down. The exhaust had started to pull the smoke up and out of the building, clearing the view on the floor. I braced my hand against the cold metal table to get my bearings. Between the smoke and urgent race to the bakery, I was feeling lightheaded. The grisly scene on the floor didn't help matters at all.

Quentin Oxley lay on his side. Blood had pooled on the side of his head that was visible. Something about his skull didn't look right. It had a large dent as if something heavy had smashed it in. A lump of dough was clutched in his hand. His pale fingers pushed into the spongy ball as if still holding it. There was no way of second guessing this. Quentin's lips had already taken on a bluish cast, and his eyes were open a slit, staring blankly at nothing.

A sudden murmur of voices and fresh air alerted me to the front door opening. The kitchen door swung open. Jack was still wearing his chef's apron. His gaze swept the kitchen and landed on the body. "So it's true," he said, trying to catch his breath. "Anna, how can I help?" He stepped into the kitchen and, once again, had to catch his breath after getting a clearer view of the victim. It took him a second to compose himself before uttering a few shaky syllables.

"Is he dead?"

"Yes. And you could help. All this smoke is from those ovens. I turned them off but it'd probably help clear the smoke faster if the trays came out. And if you could call the mainland, tell them there's been a homicide on Frostfall Island."

"Right. I'm on it." He paused and looked at me. "It's definitely a homicide?"

I waved my hand over Oxley.

Jack nodded. "Of course it is. Stupid question." He glanced around for oven mitts and set to work removing what appeared to be cake layers out of the ovens.

Now that I'd gotten over the shock and nausea of seeing Oxley with a crushed skull and a good deal of blood, I was able to take a closer look at him. Once Norwich arrived, I would be rudely dismissed and banished from anything having to do with the case. Which, of course, I would ignore entirely. However, I would not get a chance to examine the body again once the *officials* arrived. Oxley was on his side, with the right side of his head resting against the floor. The left side was the side that was caved in. His hair was matted with a great deal of blood, blood that was drying into a sticky, pasty mess. On closer inspection, I saw that there was not one dent but two in his skull. Whoever hit him, struck him more than once. It was possible the smaller dent didn't kill him right away, just a cracked skull, but his attacker made sure to finish the job. The larger, more noticeable wound had to have been almost instantly fatal. Everything else about him seemed to be unharmed. There were no cuts or bruises on his face or neck from what I could see beneath the collar of his white coat. I didn't dare touch anything on the victim because Norwich would use that as evidence that I committed the crime. He never cared if he actually had the right person as long as he had someone in custody to give him a victory.

"Jack, don't touch anything with your bare hands." He was still wearing oven mitts. He lifted them to remind me he was covered.

"Last thing I want is that foolish Norwich arresting me for murder," Jack muttered as he reached into the last oven for the blackened cake.

I pushed to my feet and pulled out my phone. If some poor unsuspecting thief ever stole my phone and managed to get into the photos, they'd be horrified. But having photos helped me solve cases long after the body had been hauled away. I took several shots at different angles. As I circled around to the other side, I noticed something odd on the ball of dough. There was an imprint, one that was mostly faded because the dough had been proofing in his dead hand. It looked like a row of small squares, but I couldn't make out more than that. I took a few close-up shots, then glanced around the kitchen to see what might have made those marks. Nothing matched the marks on the dough.

"Police have been notified," Jack said as he put away his phone. We both stared down at the lifeless body for a few seconds. "Jeez, who could have done such a thing?"

I shook my head. "As you know, he had a long list of enemies on this island and even some from across the harbor."

"Really? From across the harbor?"

"Yes, and now I have to narrow down the list because let's face it, the official they're sending us is never going to solve this case."

twenty

JACK WAS my impromptu assistant at the crime scene. After removing the burned baked goods from the oven and calling the police, he went outside to disperse the crowd while I continued my eyes only perusal of the scene. There was little else of note in the bakery. Aside from the acrid smoke residue, the front of the shop looked pleasant and laden with goodies ready to be purchased by hungry customers. Other than the grisly scene, the dead body on the floor, and the burned cakes on the cooling racks, the kitchen had none of the other hallmarks of a crime scene. There were no signs of a struggle. However, it did seem that Oxley tried to shield himself from the killer's wrath with a lump of bread dough. Uncooked sourdough loaves were heavy and would make a nice shield from whatever weapon the killer used. However, that didn't stop Oxley's assailant from striking him at least two times on the head.

I heard the front door open. I knew it couldn't be

Norwich yet. He always took his time arriving to a murder on the island. He hated the inconvenience of having to ferry across the harbor. In fact, he hated the inconvenience of the island altogether.

The kitchen door opened. I was more than a little surprised to see Nate standing in the far less smoke filled doorway. He was breathing hard. A pair of work gloves hung out of the pocket of his jeans. "Anna, you're all right."

I circled around to him. "Why wouldn't I be?"

He raked his hair back with his fingers and took a deep, steadying breath. "Word got around to the work site that the baker had killed someone. You told me you'd had words with him." He looked down at the body. "Guess the rumor, like all rumors, started as the truth and ended with a whole slab of fiction attached. I take it this is the infamous baker."

"It is. Although, *was* is the better choice of word."

While the sight on the floor was not for the sensitive, and it had certainly knocked me back at first glance, Nate approached the body without hesitation. His brows straightened, giving him a serious expression. He'd transformed from the charming, rugged construction man I'd fallen for into someone much more official. It was fun to see. I was sure he'd been quite the sight with his shoulder holster and shiny detective's badge.

"What do you see? I'm curious if you come to the same conclusion as this amateur."

Nate grinned mildly. "You're far more official and skilled than me these days." He circled around to the back of the body and crouched down to get a closer look at the smashed skull. It didn't take him long at all to recreate the murder. "Looks like he got hit once with a small but lethally heavy object. The first blow didn't do the trick, but it probably incapacitated him enough for the assailant to give his skull a second blow, the death blow. Broke right through bone."

"Well done, sir. That's exactly what I found. Anything else?" I asked, teasingly.

"I feel like I'm back in training. Hmm, let's see." He did a thorough survey of Oxley's arms, neck and shoulders. "I think that's it." He was about to lift his gaze. "Wait a minute. Something doesn't look right about that ball of dough. It's dented like the skull."

"Another gold star. The imprint has mostly disappeared now because the dough is still puffing up but—" I pulled out my phone and showed him the picture of the dough I'd taken.

Nate smelled of a mix of soap, salty air and fresh pine from the wood he'd been working with. If an aftershave company could bottle it, it would be a big seller. Or maybe it was just the right mix on Nate. "Interesting," Nate said.

"Can you tell what it is?" I asked hopefully.

"Not a clue." He glanced around the kitchen. "Whatever it is, I don't see it in this kitchen."

"Which means it was premeditated. The killer brought it with them."

"Or they took it as they left," Nate suggested.

I snapped my fingers. "Seems like the trainee has just outsmarted the trainer. You're right. Only, I do a fair amount of baking, and I can't for the life of me tell what caused this imprint. Anyhow, I'm sure you need to get back to work. As you can see, I'm fine. Oxley, on the other hand, has angered his last local."

"What about Jack?" Nate asked. "You mentioned they were feuding neighbors."

I was admittedly disappointed that he jumped right to that conclusion. "It wasn't Jack. Yes, they were having problems. As a matter of fact, Jack came in here to help me. He pulled the burned cakes out of the oven and called the police."

"Well, thank goodness for that," he said wryly.

"Oh stop. Anyhow, I'll wait outside for the illustrious Norwich to arrive. And, yes, that was a big heap of sarcasm."

Nate motioned to the side door. "Maybe the killer came in that way."

"Good guess. The front door was locked when the first customer tried to get in and find out why the bakery wasn't open. Abner Plunkett came over to see what was going on. He went through the side door and then rushed out the front door so that he wouldn't disturb any evidence. So, yes, the killer came through the side door."

"Unless they had a key and entered the front door and then locked it behind them. Then it would have to be someone with a key, a worker maybe?"

"Another possibility I didn't consider. Guess that's what years of experience gives you. Unless your name is Buckston Norwich. Speaking of which, he'll probably be here soon. I need to get out of this kitchen. The smell of stale smoke is mixing with the wholly unpleasant scent of dried blood and death. I'm starting to feel a little queasy."

Nate pulled on a work glove, and gently, without too much pressure, opened the side door. Fresh air blasted me, and I stood for a few seconds literally gulping in the clean oxygen.

"You all right?" Nate placed a supportive hand on my lower back. I always considered the gesture romantic. It showed a measure of possessiveness, healthy possessiveness, that made me feel secure.

I smiled at him. "I'm fine, and thank you for racing over here to make sure the baker didn't kill me."

The breeze ruffled his thick hair. "I have to admit, it's not easy being your boyfriend. Lots to worry about what with you starting scuffles with dastardly pastry chefs and all."

"I'll try to avoid dastardly people from this point forward, and, as for this particular one, I don't think he poses much danger anymore."

"You're right there."

We walked out from between the buildings. Earlier, Jack had sent the crowd home, letting people know there was nothing to see and that they should make room for the police to get through. They'd listened at the time, but now, word had gotten around. Probably the same completely wrong words like what Nate had heard at the work site. Regardless, people had shown up to see what was going on at the bakery.

"There she is," someone said in the crowd. "Anna, what's happened?"

"Is the baker dead?" someone else asked.

"Does that mean we can't buy croissants today?" The person asking that selfish question earned a round of disapproving groans and scowls.

Nate leaned over and kissed my cheek. "I'll leave you to your press conference."

I moved a little closer to the group that had gathered on the boardwalk. "Quentin Oxley is dead."

A collective gasp followed.

"Detective Norwich has been called." That statement was followed with a few snickers and scoffing sounds.

"You'll find out who did this, won't you, Anna?" someone asked.

"I hope so." Right then, a text came through from Frannie. "The big balding toothpick-chewing non-eagle has landed." It was Frannie's humorous way of telling me Norwich had arrived. I could almost feel his presence on the island. It always brought with it a foreboding, dark clamminess that could not be shaken until the man stepped back on the ferry to leave.

twenty-one

NORWICH HAD an entire wardrobe that was riddled with food stains. Today's sloppy ensemble had not one but two mustard spots. It wasn't even ten in the morning, and the man had been eating mustard. Actually, that sounded entirely plausible. His signature toothpick moved up and down like a tiny lever as he headed toward me with his usual glare.

"St. James, the police have arrived. Your services are no longer needed." He pulled the toothpick from his mouth for a good, loud laugh. He waved me away with his dirty fingernails. "Off with you. You're only in the way here."

After the contentious week I'd been having, mostly due to my mom's visit, I didn't have any brisk retort to offer. I was just as happy to head home with all the insider information I had regarding the victim and his many adversaries on the island. First, I needed to stop in and see Jack to make sure he was all right. It wasn't everyday you saw a dead body.

The aroma of chicken frying and biscuits baking hit me as I walked into the Pirate's Gold Restaurant. The entire place was dotted with fun, campy pirate décor. Thick, gristly ropes and patina-worn pulleys hung along the walls like nautical garland. There were even a few colorful resin parrots sitting on tables. Peggy, a woman who'd been serving tables at the restaurant for several years, looked up from the napkins she was wrapping around silverware.

"Anna, I heard what happened. Jack is positively shaken about it. How horrifying."

"Yes it is, Peggy. Is Jack in the kitchen?"

"Sure is. Go on through. I'm worried about him. Seeing you always helps."

I walked through the swinging door into the kitchen. Jack had his sleeves rolled up and an apron tied around his waist. He was rolling out biscuit dough on a work table. "Anna, how are you doing?" He wiped his hands off on a towel.

"As good as can be expected. Better now that I'm out of Norwich's presence."

Jack chuckled. "I thought the sky suddenly looked a little grayer. I suppose he'll be arresting the wrong person soon enough. I'm sure he doesn't want to tarnish his record of being spectacularly wrong at every corner."

It was my turn to laugh, and I'd really needed it. The moment of mirth was over. There was something far more serious to consider. "Jack, about Norwich and his wrongful arrests..."

"You think he might focus on me? I was thinking the same thing."

"How many people knew about the two of you feuding?" I knew I'd used the wrong word the second I said it.

"You mean how long had he been attacking my integrity as a business owner?"

I nodded. "Yes, much better put. You'll have to forgive me. It's been a long couple of days."

Jack went back to his biscuit rolling. They weren't going to bake themselves, after all. "We had a few very public, tense conversations out on the boardwalk, and there was always a line of customers standing out there. I imagine they all heard us. It would have been hard to miss."

I walked to the small kitchen window that looked out onto the boardwalk. The curious onlookers had been moved back by Norwich and his assistant. Most of them were standing in front of the restaurant now, stretching necks and standing on tiptoes to catch a glimpse of what was going on at the bakery.

I turned back to Jack. He was cutting the biscuits. He had a row of circles so he could cut six biscuits at a time, and he was fast, like a machine.

"Jack, you need to have a good, solid alibi ready." My suggestion alarmed him enough that he dropped a biscuit on the floor. I probably shouldn't have blurted it so plainly, but he needed to be ready.

"An alibi?" He pushed the fallen biscuit aside with his toe to be picked up later. "You're right, Anna. I've got to be ready for Norwich."

"Unfortunately, I know how Norwich works or, in his case, doesn't work. He'll do the least amount of investigating and question a few people before charging in with an arrest warrant. Like you said, a lot of people overheard Quentin and you arguing. What have you got? Test it out on me, and I'll let you know how to improve it."

He'd finished placing the biscuits on pans. He wiped his hands clean as he gave it some thought. "Since there were cakes burning in the oven and bread dough out on the table, I assume that means Oxley was attacked early this morning. I don't know exactly how early he arrived to start the day, but I once worked at a bread bakery, and we started at four in the morning."

"Ugh, that's early. I'd say your assumption is right. He was killed sometime between four and seven, the time the bakery normally opened."

"Well, from four until six, I was still at home in bed. Then I walked to the restaurant. I got here about 6:45 am. Oxley's customers were already lined up and waiting anxiously for the doors to open. I came in here and started chopping vegetables for the day. Then I heard the voices on the board-walk getting louder and more agitated, so I walked out to see what was going on. That was when I was told that Anna had arrived because there'd been a murder. I dashed inside to help you and then returned to my restaurant. That's my whole morning."

"So you were at home in bed," I repeated.

"And no, I don't have anyone who can confirm that." A faint blush crept up his neck. "My cat saw me, but he only cares about food, so he would never vouch for me."

We both laughed. It was a necessary break from the

serious conversation. I was very concerned that Norwich was going to focus on Jack as his prime suspect, and since Norwich couldn't be bothered to ask me if Oxley was having any other problems with people, he'd head straight to the easiest target.

Norwich's grating, somewhat nasal tone pulled me back to the little window. And there was my proof. Norwich was standing with a small group of onlookers. He was feverishly writing stuff on his notepad. The people he talked to kept glancing and pointing back at the restaurant. It was happening. Norwich was zeroing in on his single suspect. I decided not to tell Jack about the scene outside his window. He looked flustered enough as it was.

"Jack, is there anyone who might have at least seen you walk out of your house this morning? A neighbor, perhaps?"

Jack rubbed his temple. "Not that I remember. My neighbors are all late risers when the morning weather is still brisk." He looked at me. "I don't think so, Anna."

"What about when you arrived here this morning?"

"I'm the only person in the restaurant at that time of the morning, but some of the customers in line at the bakery saw me arrive. I can talk to a few of them to see if they remember me walking up." Jack poured himself a glass of water and offered me one as well. I realized then that the morning had left me quite parched. The water was cool and refreshing running down my dry throat.

"I'd get a few witnesses lined up, so you can back up your alibi. In the meantime, just be ready for Norwich's visit.

You're close by, and he doesn't like to travel or go to any lengths."

"I'll be the convenient suspect," Jack said.

"I'm afraid so, but don't worry. I'll find the real killer soon enough."

"I'm counting on it, Anna. Now, more than ever."

twenty-two

I DECIDED to make a quick stop at the 3Ts to let Sera know what had happened. I was going through a mental list of possible suspects. It seemed I'd have to use all the colored index cards in the deck. I'd add Jack to the corkboard just to be fair to the other suspects, but even if he had motive, Jack Drake was not a killer. Sera had motive too, and I'd add a card for her, but as far as I was concerned, she was already crossed off the list like Jack. My main person of interest was the man who came to the island specifically to retrieve his sourdough starter. It seemed a strange thing to travel to Frostfall for, but if it was a family treasure, as Molly had mentioned, then it was probably worth the effort. After all, it would take a hundred years to get a new one. But was sourdough starter valuable enough to prompt a murder? It sounded crazy. However, I followed enough baking blogs to know that a good sourdough starter is cared for, coddled, fed and even given a name. They were definitely revered. And, of course, I still hadn't forgotten Jamie's tight fisted tirade I witnessed early yesterday morning.

Frannie was back on the ferry. I'd been so busy I hadn't had time to check on her to see how she was feeling. She was wearing one of her many hand-knitted scarves, a bright blue one, around her neck as she ran a broom across the boat's deck.

"I see you're feeling better," I said as I approached.

She looked up from her task and adjusted the thick scarf around her neck. "I am, although not a hundred percent. Now Joe has whatever bug I had, and you know how much worse it is for the men folk when they're feeling under the weather. I still had to make dinner, clean dishes, take care of the dogs. He tucked himself deep into the bed quilts, and I don't have to go home to know that he hasn't left those blankets all day."

"I'm glad to see you back on the boat."

"It's been quite a week so far. I heard murmurs on the wharf that something had happened over at the bakery. When that toothpick-gnawing turtle without a shell stepped onto my boat this morning, I knew it was something big. Boy, I have one sore throat and the whole island falls apart."

"It's true, and that means you should always take good care of yourself. I did want to ask you if you happened to see a man leaving the island today. He's slightly above average in height with very dark hair, and when I saw him, he was wearing a black coat and dark hat. Sorry I don't have anything more specific than that."

"Doesn't sound familiar. Do you think he's the killer?"

"Too early in my investigation to know for sure, but if you haven't seen anyone matching that description, then I'll assume he's still on the island."

"The ferry hasn't been too busy, so I think I'd remember if I saw him. I did see something interesting this morning after my return from the mainland. I was puttering into dock. Jamie Baxter had already unloaded his catch, and he was back in his slip at the harbor. I spotted his girlfriend, Remi, standing just outside his boat. She was crying. It almost looked as if she was pleading with him about something. Couldn't hear the words over my noisy engine, but whatever she was asking him, he wasn't having any of it. He waved her away and turned his back to her to work on his nets. I guess there must be trouble in paradise."

"Sounds like that might be the case." While I often discussed my investigations and evidence with my small Moon River family, I avoided starting any rumors elsewhere on the island. Frannie was a good friend, but she also had the ear of just about anyone who crossed the harbor. I didn't want her to know about Jamie and Remi's troubles and how they were connected to the dead baker.

"Where are you off to now?" Fran asked.

"I thought I'd drop by and see Sera."

"I'll bet this won't be terrible news for Sera." Frannie covered her mouth. "Jeez, that's awful to say." She shrugged. "But then it's true, so how bad can it be?" You could always count on Fran to be straight talking like a boat captain. "Sera's business took a big hit once the bakery opened and word got around that the breads and pastries were delicious.

The closest thing any of us have to a bakery and fresh bread is Luigi's Italian Bakery, and that's a harbor cruise and a twenty mile bus ride inland. I told Sera I thought the novelty would eventually wear off, but it seems that novelty has ended altogether."

"I know she was worried about her business. Although, this is a dreadful way to win back customers. I'm sure Sera will be just as shocked as the rest of us. I'll get going. It's good to see you back, and if you could—"

"Keep an eye out for the suspect?" She saluted me. "I'm on duty, and I'll report it immediately."

I waved and walked briskly to Sera's shop. There were far more people inside the 3Ts and out at the tables than the day before, and there was plenty of tittle-tattle going on. The murmurs were easy to interpret. Everyone was talking about the murder. Sera was rushing around, pouring tea and serving tarts. There was no sign of Cora.

Samuel came out of the kitchen wearing blue checked oven mitts. "Hey, Anna. We got hit with a big rush that we weren't expecting, and now we're playing catch up in the kitchen." He scanned the room for Sera and found her in the back corner placing two tarts down in front of customers. "Hey, Sera, I pulled out the tray of Gouda quiches. Are the lemon custard tarts ready to go in?"

"Yes, and make sure you don't slosh them around." Sera spotted me. "Anna, hello. As you can see, your sister didn't make it in. Something about a headache. I think she worried I was going to make her do more cleaning, but, as you see, we're back to business with tarts and tea."

We walked together up to the counter, and I sat on my stool. "I assume you've heard the news," I said.

Sera tried to look upset. She wasn't going to win any awards for her act. "Horrible, of course, but with the way that man was making enemies on this island, I'm not that surprised. Well, maybe a little surprised. I didn't realize he'd pushed someone to murder. Do you have any of the details?"

I shook my head. "I have some, but I've got to arrange them in my mind first. Norwich is here."

"Ah, I thought I smelled a certain odor in the air."

We both had a good laugh, then Sera's eyes rounded. "You don't think he'll come here to talk to me? After all, everyone on the island knew that my business had slowed to a crawl. I'd told more than one person that I might have to shut down. I did that mainly to gain some sympathy and support from our very fickle island residents. I was hoping word would get around and people would return in fear that they'd lose their favorite tea shop. This place is sort of the local pub of the island village."

"Only instead of pints of ale you sell cups of chai. I agree. This is the local watering hole, the place where everyone comes to talk to each other and exchange Frostfall gossip. It's a shame people didn't feel more loyalty to the place." I glanced around. Two thirds of the tables were filled, and with an early morning murder, there was plenty of gossip to go around. "At least they're back now. I guess everyone's had their last chocolate croissant for awhile."

"Did you want a cup of tea?" Sera asked.

"No, you're busy, so I'll head off. I just wanted to tell you the news. It was silly of me considering you own a place that literally has tittle-tattle in the name." I patted the counter. "I'm glad to see the tarts and tea flowing again. I'll keep you posted."

"Please do."

I headed out of the tea shop and turned toward the museum. I hadn't spoken to Abner since he showed me to the gory scene in the bakery kitchen. I needed to check in on him and find out if there was anything else he remembered from the last few days that seemed out of the ordinary. With any luck, he'd seen the sourdough stranger.

twenty-three

IT WAS SHAPING up to be a nice day with a few wispy clouds and mostly blue sky. Each day farther into spring brought more color to the island. Soon, the yellows of the seaside goldenrod, the smoky blues of the chicory and hot pinks of the swamp roses would make us all forget about the long, monochrome winter. A line of seagulls waited patiently along the back of a bench across from the bakery. They'd already discovered that that particular stretch of boardwalk was the place to go for crumbs of baked goods. However, not today. They were sticking it out, it seemed, but they didn't look too happy with the way the morning was going. Norwich had apparently cleared the area so that the coroner could take over the crime scene. A gurney with an empty black bag sat outside the side door between the museum and the bakery. I'd have to give a call to my friend, Mindy, at the precinct. Since I was not *officially* on the case, Mindy was a good secret source for details concerning murder investigations. However, it wasn't going to take much examination to discover the cause of death this round. Oxley's head wounds had been traumatic. The violence of the attack indicated the assailant was extremely mad. After meeting the man personally, I knew firsthand that he was arrogant and liked to goad people into anger. I was sure he'd used that bullying, cruel attitude to get ahead in life. Some people thought being ruthless was the only way to be successful. In the end, it turned out to be his downfall.

I was relieved not to see Norwich on my way past the bakery to the museum. He was just like Oxley in his interactions with others. He was a genuine bully. The less interactions with him the better.

Abner was sitting behind his desk in the tiny reception area of the museum. He was scheduling out museum events on a big calendar. An impressive model of Blackbeard's infamous *Queen Anne's Revenge* sat in a glass case across from his desk. A long string of pirate flags hung above it. It had been decided long before I was a Frostfall resident, even long before I'd ever heard of the place, that the island's historic heritage would be rich in pirate lore. There was no actual proof of this buccaneer history, but the plan had helped put Frostfall on a list of favorite Atlantic coast tourist stops.

"How are you doing, Abner?" I asked.

He placed down his pen and walked around to the front of his desk. "Honestly, I'm still a bit shaken, but I'll be fine. Are you on the case?" He winked.

"I think I better get a jump on it before Norwich makes his usual clumsy mess of things. I was hoping you could help me. Tuesday morning, I was out for one of my predawn walks, and I came this direction. I spotted a man I'd never seen before. He was fairly tall and wearing a dark coat and hat. I couldn't see him too well because he was standing in the shadows of the museum."

Abner was nodding energetically before I finished. "Yes, odd man with dark hair and sharp features. I've never seen him on the island."

"Where did you see him?"

"Right here in the museum. It was on Monday. He bought a ticket. I was keeping a close eye on him because he was acting strangely."

I had to tamp down my excitement. Had I already found the killer? That would sure put Norwich in his place. "How is that?"

"Once the man walked into the center display room, rather than peruse the exhibits, he kept strolling to the window."

The main display room had been set up to look like the interior of a pirate ship complete with sleeping pirates in the bunks and a captain's table set for dinner. I knew there was a window on each side of the room. One looked toward the other shops and Tobias' accounting office. The other looked out into the alley between the museum and the bakery. It was easy to guess which window had his interest.

"Was he at the window that looks out at the bakery?"

"Yes, he was. It was strange because all you can see from that window is the side door to the bak—" Abner's eyes practically bulged with comprehension. "Was that him? Was the killer standing right inside this museum? Was he—what's the phrase the police use?"

"You mean, was he casing the joint? Or in this case, the bakery? I think he might have been. Still, it's early in the investigation. I'm just trying to gather information."

Abner clapped once. "I saw him another time." He seemed to be enjoying this. "Oh my gosh, I can't believe I didn't think of this until now. It might just be the—" he paused. "What's the other phrase they use when a piece of crucial evidence is discovered?"

"Do you mean the smoking gun?"

Abner snapped his fingers. "Yes, that's it. The smoking gun."

This was going far better than I expected. I moved closer and straightened to attention to let him know I was all ears. Maybe, I wouldn't even have to pull out the corkboards. Maybe, for a change, this one was done before it really started.

"Last night, I stayed late to work on some flyers for the summer events. When I locked up, I saw that same man come out from the alley between the two buildings. I asked if I could help him, but he ignored me and hurried away."

"You're sure it was the same man?"

Abner's eyes were glittering with excitement. "Absolutely. Have I helped the case? Do we have our killer?"

I couldn't stop a smile. He'd placed himself unofficially on the team. Frankly, his information was good enough that he deserved the title of team member.

"What you've told me is quite significant, Abner. We now

know that the sourdough stranger—" I'd inadvertently used my nickname.

Abner's brows bunched up. "Did you just call him the sourdough stranger?"

"At the moment, he's nameless, and sourdough stranger is easier than taller than average with dark hair and a dark hat."

"But why sourdough?" he asked.

"That's right. I haven't told you what *I* know about the man. I overheard him in a contentious conversation with Quentin in that very same alleyway. It seemed the man was here to reclaim his family's treasure, a century-old sourdough starter."

Poor Abner looked even more confused. "Is that a thing? A century old?"

"Yes, sourdough starters can last forever if they're taken care of properly. With time, they provide more flavor. And each one is unique, so a good starter is highly coveted."

"So the man was accusing Quentin of stealing his sour-dough starter?" He scratched his head. "Seems like a silly thing to kill someone over."

"I agree, but maybe there's more to the story. And if Quentin had the starter, which I think might have been the case, he made it clear to the man that he had no intention of handing it back."

Abner grinned. "My goodness I had no idea a case like this could be so intriguing. It seems you have your work cut out for you. Do you know where to find this man, the one looking for his sourdough starter?" He chuckled lightly. "I don't know when I've ever used that exact phrase before, and I doubt I'll ever use it again."

"I must say, the sourdough motive is a first for me as well. Thanks so much for your help, Abner. I'll keep you posted."

He walked me to the door. "Please do, and if I see the man, I'll call you immediately."

I had people looking out for the stranger, but it was really Fran's eyes that mattered. Unless the man came on his own boat, the only way off the island was on the *Salty Bottom*. Hopefully, he'd show up soon.

twenty-four

WINSTON'S PARADE OF VULNERABLE, sweet rescue animals had pushed us to the collective decision to eat vegetarian. I'd come up with my own substitute for burgers. It was a mixture of sautéed mushrooms, brown rice, black beans and a good deal of seasoning. The group loved them, especially when I cooked my homemade, seasoned potato wedges to go with the burgers. I'd found homemade burger buns were a snap to make and added to the tastiness of the meal.

I was just finishing shaping the buns for baking when Cora came downstairs. Her face had that droopy expression she always wore when something wasn't going right. I knew this time the frown had to do with the departure of a certain man.

"You knew he was only going to be here a few days," I said as I brushed milk on the tops of the buns to make them golden.

"Who?"

I turned back with a raised brow. "Seriously, you've already forgotten Arlo? You made a big scene this morning. I assume that same scene caused you to take the day off. By the way, Sera's business was booming today."

"Darn. I probably missed out on some good tips. Yes, it's true. I was upset this morning. It was nice to meet someone new. This island is rather limited in eligible bachelors."

"But you're no longer thinking about Arlo?" I asked.

Cora shrugged. I'd seen the same shrug many times over men. She always had so many of them nipping at her heels, it was never a big deal when one faded away. "He was fun. A nice diversion. I'm sad Mom's leaving tomorrow. I thought she might stick around for awhile. I was just upstairs helping her pack."

Daughter guilt gripped me. Cora was wearing a genuine frown about Mom leaving, and inside my head there was a small party. It meant things would get back to normal again. Worry gripped me too.

"Cora, you're not thinking of moving back to the city, are you? It seems that was Mom's big reason for her impromptu visit."

Cora sighed. "I don't know. She has a point about it being nearly impossible for me to meet someone here on the island. Arlo's visit sort of reinforced that. Still, I'm happier here than I've been in a long time. And I do love my job."

"And?" I prodded and gave her a serious head tilt.

"And I like being with my sister again. Now, if you could

just arrange for a handsome, single billionaire to move to Frostfall Island, I'd be pleased as a peach."

"I can't make any promises on the billionaire. And, for what it's worth, I'd miss not having you around."

"Thanks, *Annie-poo*." She laughed as she got up from the table. "I forgot about that horrible nickname."

"Not me. It's etched into my pre-teen psyche along with my first pimple and my first school dance where I joined a long list of tragic historical figures known as wallflowers."

Cora was still having a good laugh as she walked out of the kitchen. Seconds later, the back door opened and Nate walked in, his silver lunch pail hanging from his hand and his work boots edged in sandy dirt.

Nate placed the lunch pail down near the door, so he could free his hands up to greet Huck. (Yes, the dog was always the first to receive a hello and a hug, but I didn't mind. It was one of the things I liked about Nate.)

Spring was just beginning, but Nate had already lost the paleness brought on by a long winter. His skin had a fresh glowing tan that made his blue eyes sparkle. "How did the rest of your day go?" He walked over and kissed my cheek. "Sorry I can't give you a better hello, but I'm covered with grime and sweat. There's no denying that the sun has moved back to our side of the planet."

"My day has been interesting. Norwich arrived."

"That's too bad," he quipped.

"I agree. I'm going to be pulling out the good old corkboards after dinner. You're invited to join me as I write out my suspect cards. There'll be a few, as is usually the case when the victim is particularly unlikable, and Quentin Oxley went out of his way to rile people."

"Who do you think Norwich's next victim will be? And by victim, I mean the next innocent person to be put through a humiliating arrest for a crime they didn't commit?"

The timer rang. I pulled the freshly baked burger buns out of the oven and placed them on the cooling rack. "Honestly, I'm not entirely sure. However, I did tell Jack to be ready with his alibi. The customer line for the bakery trailed all the way down to his restaurant. Many people were witness to the two men arguing about which direction smells were flowing. Norwich was talking to some of those people this morning."

"Does Jack have a good alibi?" Nate poured himself a glass of cold milk.

"Not really. I think the murder took place in the very early hours, between four and seven. Jack, like most of us, was still at home in bed."

Nate gulped half the glass of milk and sighed with satisfaction. "So good. Who is the *real* detective on the case looking at as a main suspect?"

It was hard not to smile at being referred to as the real detective. "I'm focused on the stranger whose sole purpose for coming to the island was to retrieve his family's sourdough starter."

Nate choked a little on the next sip. He coughed a few times until the milk cleared his throat. "Did you say a sourdough starter?"

"I did. You have to know something about sourdough to understand, so you'll just have to trust me on that."

He put up his hand to show he accepted the terms of agreement. "I'm certainly not one to question the methods and motives of the world's greatest island detective."

I couldn't stop the smile again. "World's greatest? I kind of like that."

"And most beautiful," he added with a flirty grin.

"Yes? Go on."

"And she's pretty handy with her hamburger buns too."

My shoulders dropped. "Should have stopped while I was ahead."

"Yeah, me too." Nate combed his hair back with fingers. "I've got sand everywhere. I'm going to go up and take a shower before dinner."

"Probably a good idea. I'm going to take out my corkboards."

Nate left the kitchen. I headed to the closet and pulled out the corkboards to hang on the wall. I would wait before I printed and pinned up the photos of the victim. This was a particularly grisly death, so it was possible I wouldn't hang them up at all. Everyone in the house was used to seeing my crime scene photos, but a dented skull was particularly hard to look at.

This was going to be a two corkboard case. I was hanging the second board when Mom came into the kitchen. "Did Cora tell you I'm leaving tomorrow?"

"Yes, we're sorry to see you go so soon." I thought I'd sounded convincing, but Mom wasn't buying it.

"You know this island is too small for me. Island fever, isn't that what they call it?"

"It is but it generally takes longer than two days for it to take hold."

Mom came over to me. I thought she was going to hug me, a rarity for us. It continued as a rare event. She reached up and wiped her finger across my forehead. "You had a streak of flour on your face." Her gaze swept over the tray of buns. "Those smell wonderful, but I don't understand why you go through so much trouble. You could just buy a pack of hamburger buns at the market."

"I enjoy making things from scratch. They taste better, and the people who live in this house appreciate it. I think I have a pack of buns in the freezer if you'd prefer to eat your burger on a store-bought bun." It seemed I was on the defense even more than usual this trip but then she'd been pretty relentlessly Mom-ish the entire visit.

Her mouth twisted like she'd bit a lemon. "I'm just trying to be helpful. You're tied to this kitchen all day. I don't know how you can bear it."

"I'm not tied to this kitchen, and I happen to enjoy baking and cooking. You spend your spare time shopping for new purses and shoes, and I spend mine in the kitchen preparing food that makes people happy."

"I should hope so. Fresh hamburger buns and biscuits and cookies. Who wouldn't be happy about that?" She glanced around. "Where's the ground beef? I can help you shape the hamburger patties."

"Patties are made and cooling in the refrigerator, but

they're not made of ground beef. As you know, we eat vege-tarian foods in this house."

She laughed. "Certainly not all the time."

"Yes, all the time. I promise you'll like these burgers. Now, if you don't mind, I've got to cut some tomatoes and red onions." I lifted the colander of washed veggies from the sink.

"I was really hoping Cora would be going with me when I left," Mom said sadly.

"So, your little plot didn't work. I'm glad. Cora is happy here. She's a grown woman. Let her make her own decisions."

"Don't get so angry. I just think I know what's best for my children, even if they ignore my advice."

I sliced the first tomato with more speed and force than usual. "I'm not angry, Mom." I'd pictured a much more relaxing dinner making session where I could start theorizing about the murder. (Yes, a murder case was more relaxing than a conversation with my mom.)

"Fine, but I'm your mother, and I know anger when I see it. I'm going up to finish packing. I'm sure you'll be glad to see the backside of me."

I put down the knife and turned around.

"Mom, if you would just come to visit without an agenda, without some evil plan to lure Cora away from the island. If you'd have come here to—" I stopped. "Never mind." I spun back around. I was hoping to hear her footsteps leaving. Instead, she came back into the kitchen.

"Of course, I came here to see you, Anna. It's just you

don't ever seem happy to see me. Cora is always glad to see her mom, but you just put up your defenses and work hard to keep me at an arm's distance."

Unexpectedly, her words caused tears to well up in my eyes. I turned back toward her. "Mom, if you could step out of yourself for a second and become the proverbial fly on the wall, you might see that you're an entirely different Mom to Cora than you are to me."

She stood silently for a second, absorbing what I said. At least, I hoped that was the case.

"Annie-poo, that's because you are entirely different people. Cora has one thing to offer the world—her beauty. But you have so many complicated layers. If I'm harder on you it's because I know there's so much there, so much potential, so much to offer." She walked forward, and with some reluctance, I moved into her embrace. We hugged for a long time.

"Mom," I said over her shoulder. "You underestimate Cora if you think she only has beauty. Customers at the tea shop adore her. Yes, part of that is because she looks like Grace Kelly and dresses like a Hollywood starlet, but mostly, it's her charm and humor." We dropped our arms. I smiled up at her. "She has way more to offer than beauty. She's happy here right now. Let her do this. Let her find her own future."

Mom wiped a tear from the corner of her eye. "You're right, Annie-poo." She paused. "I'm sorry. Anna. I guess you've outgrown Annie-poo."

"Yep. I think I outgrew it when I was seven, but for what

it's worth, I don't mind it all that much. As long as there are no other people in the room."

She laughed and we hugged again.

"Now, about that extremely handsome tenant of yours. I'm an old lady who doesn't have much radar for these things anymore, but I think he might have a little thing for you."

"You think?"

"I think so."

"Interesting." It was hard to hold back a smile. "Mom, I really am sorry you're leaving already. I hope you come back again soon."

twenty-five

WE'D all sat down to homemade veggie burgers and lemon shortbread dessert. Winston was working late, but we all knew that was mostly code for I'm staying with Alyssa. We saw him less and less, which was to be expected with a budding romance. My mom said she had no interest in or stomach for a murder investigation. When Opal mentioned she had *Breakfast at Tiffany's* cued up on her television, my mom decided to join her for the movie. That left Tobias, Cora and Nate for the corkboard session. Tobias had a keen interest in the case because the murder happened just yards from his office. He'd been witness to the constant flow of troubles Oxley had caused in his short time on the island. Cora was mostly staying because she'd napped during the day and was too wide awake to even consider bed. Nate, on the other hand, looked weary from a long day on the construction site, particularly because he was up before dawn to see Arlo off. Still, he insisted he was interested in talking about the case. I was sure it was an amateurish endeavor compared to the process he used when he was a detective. He'd insisted, several times, I did a lot better job than some of the people he'd worked with.

I stood up at the boards like a teacher about to present a lesson. "Thank you for joining me on this brainstorm session. We have one dead victim—Quentin Oxley. I didn't print out the photos of his body because I wasn't sure you guys would appreciate looking at them."

"Abner mentioned it was quite a terrible scene this morning." Tobias was working on his third piece of lemon shortbread.

Cora sat up with interest. "Really? What happened? Did someone pour hot oil on him or suffocate him with bread dough? Was he beaten to death with a rolling pin?"

"Not quite," I said. "And very specific examples, I must say. Oxley was hit in the head with a heavy object—twice. One of the blows, the second, mostly likely, was fatal. It caved in his skull."

"Ew, was there brainage?" Cora asked. "You know drainage of brain matter?"

"Yes, I got that. I didn't look specifically for brain matter."

Tobias crinkled his face and pushed the dessert plate away.

"Any word yet on what weapon was used in the attack?" Nate asked.

"No, I'm going to call my friend Mindy at the station tomorrow to see if she can get me some specifics. According to my calculations, Oxley died between four and seven in the morning. He was working alone in the bakery." I pinned the card with the murder details onto the first board.

"Yesterday, there was quite the scene outside the bakery at closing." Tobias had resumed his shortbread nibbling.

"I was hoping you had some good insight to add to this, Toby. What happened?"

"Sally Hogan had been running the bakery counter all by herself. I went in there a few times, and she was always harried and trying to keep up with customers. I was sitting in my office going over some numbers on an account when I heard shouting outside. I walked to the window. Sally Hogan was standing with one fist on her hip and the other hand pointing angrily at Quentin. My office has double-glazed windows, but Sally was talking loudly. I heard her mention something about being overworked and taken for granted. That was certainly what I noticed when I was inside the bakery. One morning, poor Sally was busy filling a large box with a dozen pastries. The shop was filled to capacity, and there was a long line trailing out the door. Oxley had the nerve to stick his head out from the kitchen to yell at her for not moving customers along faster. My phone rang so I missed the end of their conversation outside the window, but I heard later that Sally was no longer going to work at the bakery."

"Was she fired or did she quit?" Nate asked.

"I'm not sure."

"Thanks for that, Toby." I picked up a pink card and wrote down Sally's name and her relationship to the victim. I looked up at the group. "Motive would be anger due to Quentin being a terrible boss?"

"Sounds like it to me," Cora said. "Who'd ever work for someone like that? Speaking of bosses, of course, I have great ones, but if you're going by motive..."

I nodded and picked up a green card. "I'm putting Sera's name on the card, but you can never, ever tell her."

Nate chuckled. "It's always awkward when you have to consider a friend or acquaintance a suspect. I've had to do it myself. I don't think Sera and Samuel had anything to do with Oxley's death, but they might have had the best motive of all."

"Business was positively dead," Cora said. "Sera was worried she'd have to close the shop."

I wrote Sera's name extra small on the card and pinned it to the board.

"And then there was the trouble Jack Drake was having with his neighbor," Nate, a little too gleefully, reminded me. "If Sera and Samuel are up there—"

I pulled out a yellow card. "I was going to add his name," I said curtly. "I'm just getting to it. But I think we can add it with the same caveat that Jack didn't do it."

"Never count out anyone," Nate added. "Detective 101."

I ignored his comment and added Jack's name to the board.

I pulled a blue card out. "This one is for the mystery suspect, the man who wants back his sourdough starter."

Tobias sat forward with pinched brows. "Did you say a sourdough starter?"

"Yes, I did and I don't want to explain it, but trust me, there is value in a sourdough starter. Just think of it as an antique that gets more valuable with age. Anyhow, this suspect has been seen lurking around the bakery on more than one occasion, and he spoke with Quentin. They had a strong exchange of words. Quentin would not return the starter. Frannie said she hasn't seen a man matching his description leaving the island. My theory is that he's sticking around because he hasn't found the starter yet." I pinned the mystery man card to the board.

"I was at the crime scene with you this morning," Nate said. "If the killer was looking for the sourdough starter, it seems like some of the cupboards and drawers would have been open. Generally, when someone is looking for something frantically, like after they've killed someone, they rummage through stuff quickly. They never close the cupboards or drawers back up."

I felt my entire posture deflate. "I hadn't thought of that. Guess I need more years of experience."

Nate shrugged and added in a cocky grin.

Cora yawned. Only she could make a yawn look elegant. "I think that's it for me. The sleepies have finally hit. I'm going up for a bubble bath and bed. Good luck with the case."

"She lasted longer than usual," Tobias pointed out.

"True." I plucked a white card from the pack. "Now, I'm going to add Murray Hogan to the board because he was extremely mad at Quentin for treating Sally so poorly. That leaves the last cards for my final two suspects. Now the motive switches to the tried and true one—jealousy. Remi Seymour has been seeing Jamie Baxter, the fisherman, for at least a year. But I saw Remi hanging around the bakery and flirting heavily with Quentin. I also witnessed Jamie pounding on the door of the bakery very early one morning. He was filled with rage."

Nate sat forward. "Maybe you should star Jamie's card. Whoever hit Oxley was filled with rage. I saw the victim's head. That was not a gentle pat. There was an explosive amount of anger behind it."

"Good point." I starred Jamie's card and pinned it to the board. I put one up for Remi, as well, only because it seemed she was more upset with Quentin than smitten the last time I saw her. The boards were crowded, and I hadn't even pinned up any photos. I stood back and looked at the array of colored cards. "Wow. This is what happens when you walk around all day with a chip on your shoulder. You get a lot of suspects in your murder case."

"Looks like you've got your work cut out for you." Tobias said.

"Sure looks that way, Toby. I was afraid that might be the case."

twenty-six

THE NEW MORNING sun was just being born as Huck and I moved quickly along the north end of Island Drive. I'd decided to leave my paints at home for the morning and travel out on bicycle. My feet could only carry me so far before I had to turn around to get breakfast started. On wheels, I could easily make it all the way around Calico Peak and back. The snow pack from the top of the peak was melting and dripping down the sides of the small mountain like ice cream melting down an upside down cone. Huck was thrilled to see a whole new set of squirrels to chase. The ones that lived near the boarding house were already wise to his antics. They knew to stay aloft on the highest branches whenever they saw or heard him. The squirrels at the north end of the island were far less Huck-savvy.

Pedaling uphill had certainly kick-started my engine for the day. And I needed the boost. According to the collage of color on the corkboards, I had a complex case in front of me.

If I was being honest with myself, I was confused about where to start. Nate had thrown a solid wrench into my theory that the mystery man was the killer. If he'd killed Quentin to retrieve his sourdough starter, then why wasn't the kitchen in disarray? Unless the starter was sitting on the work island in plain view. Then he wouldn't have needed to rummage through cupboards and drawers. If Quentin hadn't been expecting the man, which I could only assume was the case, then he might have left the starter out on the counter. That was where I kept mine when I was feeding it and getting it ready to use in bread. What if the man killed Quentin and then panicked and fled the bakery afraid he'd be caught? That would explain why Frannie hadn't seen him leave the island. He was still trying to get that starter.

I reached a spot on the island that afforded a nice view of the harbor. Fishing boats were burping out diesel as they headed out toward open waters. They looked small, almost like toy boats as they coasted over the morning ripples. The unexpected visitors and even more unexpected murder hadn't allowed me any time to dwell on the wedding photo with the woman from Michael's past hovering creepily in the background. It was yet another unsettling event. On my fortieth birthday, I'd received a card from someone who knew it was my birthday. The card was unsigned and contained a sprig of dried purple larkspur, a flower I just happened to have in my bridal bouquet. I never found out who the card was from. Then there were the odd sensations I occasionally experienced when I felt as if someone was watching me while out on the island. Huck seemed to have the same experiences. Occasionally, he'd bark at something, but when I checked nothing was there. I'd even on one occasion convinced myself I smelled the pipe tobacco Michael used to smoke. I'd been working hard to dismiss the episodes as my imagination. (Except the card. That was far too real to dismiss and still a mystery.) But the wedding photo had added a new layer to everything.

A few explanations had crept up in my attempt to explain her presence, but none of them were good. If Michael had invited her without telling me, then I would have to ask why. Only, I'd never get that answer because Michael was gone. If she was stalking him, then did she have something to do with his disappearance? There were too many questions, and it seemed I was never going to know the answers. I'd considered for all of two minutes looking up Denise to ask her why she was in my wedding photo, but self-preservation kept me from doing it. After all the heartbreak I'd gone through from losing Michael, the last thing I needed was to discover that he'd been having an affair with his high school sweetheart during our entire courtship.

My phone rang, jarring me from my thoughts. (Which was for the best.) It was early for a phone call. I expected it to be Cora asking me where the new toothpaste was or letting me know the hot water ran out during her shower. She always informed me of that inconvenience as if there was something I could do about it. It wasn't Cora.

"Hey, Jack, is everything all right?" I asked. It was highly unusual for him to call me, let alone call me at the break of dawn.

I sensed that he was pacing because heavy footsteps and breathing rumbled through the phone. "No, things are not all right. That imbecile of a detective knocked on my door before the sun was even up. He barreled inside and started firing off dozens of questions about where I was the morning of the murder and why did I hate Quentin Oxley so much and did I ever threaten to kill him? All crazy stuff."

"Unfortunately, Jack, that's how Norwich conducts an investigation."

"Well, it's pretty obvious I'm his prime suspect. He said as much."

"But he didn't arrest you. That's a good sign. Maybe after so many mishaps, he's decided to take his time before making an arrest."

"What am I going to do, Anna? I know how these things work. If he arrests me, even if I'm entirely innocent and get released the next day, the arrest will stick with everyone. People on this island will never look at me the same. They'll look at me as the guy in a fake pirate hat who was once arrested for murder." The distress in his voice was hard to hear.

"Jack, try not to worry. I'm working on the case. Now that I know your reputation is on the line, I'll try my hardest to solve it today." I knew I was making a bold promise, but this time, I really was racing against the clock. Jack was right. If Norwich hauled him away in handcuffs that would be the only thing people remembered. If only the official detective on the case wasn't such a complete and utter fool, I wouldn't have to worry about him arresting a good friend.

"I sure hope you can figure this out. I'm counting on you, Anna."

"I'll do my best, Jack. Talk to you later."

I took a deep breath and gazed back out at the harbor. "Right, no pressure, Anna. Just solve the multi-suspect case in the next twelve hours."

twenty-seven

MY MIND WASN'T FOCUSED on breakfast, and I managed to burn four English muffins. It was my mom's good-bye breakfast, but I just didn't have the time for anything fancy like Eggs Benedict or cheese omelets. I opted for breakfast sandwiches—egg patties and cheese between buttery English muffins. I'd pushed open the kitchen window to get rid of the burnt toast smell, but every single person who came down to breakfast asked me the same question. "What's burning?" So when Tobias walked in from his morning swim and uttered the same two words, I snapped.

"English muffins, Toby. I forgot them and they burned and now everyone here is clear that I messed up." The second my ridiculous rant ended, my heart sank. Tobias looked hurt. "I'm sorry, Toby. That was uncalled for. It's just everyone has asked me the same question this morning, and you were on the receiving end of my pent up frustration."

Tobias smiled weakly and nodded. "I'll be right down for breakfast. It looks delicious."

Nate had gobbled down his sandwich in seconds and was already picking up his lunch. He winked at me. "It's good to blow off steam sometimes," he said quietly. "Rhonda, it's been a pleasure. Hope to see you again soon."

Mom blushed and smiled and fidgeted with her napkin. "It was so nice meeting you, Nate." I half expected her to blow him a kiss on his way out the door.

It seemed I hadn't been the only one to notice the fluttery school girl reaction to Nate's very average good-bye. Everyone was staring at her. Opal and Cora were trying hard but failing to hide their amusement.

Mom seemed to suddenly realize she'd made a bit of a scene and blushed again.

"It's all right, Rhonda," Opal said. "You should have seen Cora's and my reaction when that boy walked into the boarding house for the first time." Opal and my mom had bonded during my mom's short stay. I sensed that Opal was going to miss her.

"Right, then," Mom said briskly, happy to change the subject. "When should we leave? I don't want to miss the next ferry."

"You've got time, Mom, but I'll walk you there as soon as breakfast is cleaned up. Cora, are you working today?" I sat down to eat my breakfast. After the toaster fiasco I was short muffins, so I ate the egg patty with cheese, no muffin.

"Yes," Cora said grumpily. "I was enjoying the time off, but Sera said business is buzzing again."

Mom smiled at Cora over her coffee cup. I knew what was coming. "Well, Cora, dear, you could always head back to the city with me. I've got a very nice modern apartment. No creaks or drafts like this house."

It seemed our mother daughter moment had been fleeting. I'd hoped Mom had given up on the idea of coaxing Cora back to the mainland, but that was me being naïve. Mom never gave up on something she wanted. She was relentless. Granted, that same kind of determination got her through life pretty well. I just wished she'd leave my sister off her list of goals.

"But I'd have to work there too," Cora reminded her. "And I do like my job here. I was just getting pulled into that lazy bones mode, like we used to get in summer after school had been out for a month."

I laughed. "Remember we wouldn't even get out of bed. We'd run to the kitchen, fill bowls with Sugar Pops and then eat the cereal in bed. Ah, those were the days. No worries. No stress—"

"And thighs that didn't rub together no matter how much Sugar Pops you consumed," Cora added with a dreamy sigh.

Tobias had returned from his morning shower just as Cora mentioned thighs rubbing together. He blushed and made a mumbling excuse about having to eat breakfast on the go because he had so much work today.

It was just us women sitting at the table. The colorful corkboards hung behind Opal's head. They reminded me of the difficult task ahead. I would start the only place I knew to start. Back at the scene of the crime. I doubted that Norwich did a thorough evidence search. It was too much work for the man. With any luck, something got left behind. Something that would help me find the killer.

Cora had removed the muffin and most of the cheese so she could just eat the egg. I was sure it had to do with her recent moaning and groaning about how her clothes were all too tight. It meant I could have had a muffin with my eggs but then my pants were a little snug too.

"I forgot to tell you," Cora started. "This morning, when Sera phoned to make sure I was coming in for my shift, she sounded sort of grumpy. I asked her what was wrong. Turns out that detective stopped by her shop this morning. He told her that he'd heard from people that her tea shop was going under because the bakery was so popular. He grilled her on her whereabouts during the time of the murder. Of course, she and Samuel were at home. They usually get to work about five to start the tarts. But since business had been so slow, they weren't getting in until later. The detective told them they were on his person's of interest list and that he'd be back to talk to them. And get this—he told them not to leave the island or the country. Naturally, both Samuel and Sera were really upset by the visit."

"Who can blame them?" Opal sprinkled more sugar in her coffee. She practically drank it like a syrup.

"This case is extra stressful." I got up to clear dishes. I needed to get moving. "I'm racing against a completely incompetent detective to find the real killer before he embarrasses good friends and island locals with false arrests." I put the dishes in the sink. They'd have to wait. Norwich was on a roll, and he didn't care who he ran over in his clumsy pursuit of justice. "Mom, if you're all packed up, we can start our journey to the harbor."

twenty-eight

CORA WALKED with us to the dock to see mom off. I hugged Mom and told her to come back soon. (I worked very hard to sound sincere and thought I did an admirable job.) Cora and Mom made a bit more of a scene with tears and sobs as if they were parting forever. Then the three St. James women walked in three different directions; Mom toward the ferry, Cora toward the 3Ts and me toward the bakery.

The day was a little colder than normal, and some dreary clouds had moved over the island, blotting out the warmth of the sun. At least it wasn't raining. Although, the air felt heavy with the threat of an afternoon drizzle. I picked up my pace only to realize my legs were a little wobbly from the early morning bike ride. I had too much to do. I couldn't stroll slowly around town. Maybe I'd even pick up my bike after the trip back to the crime scene. It would help me get around faster. Now that Norwich had not one but three of my good friends in his sights, I needed to make quick work of the case.

Everything seemed back to the way it was pre-Quentin Oxley. Jack's staff was busy readying the indoor and outdoor dining areas for the day's lunch crowd. The rich aromas flowing out of the vents on top of the restaurant signaled that lunch menu prep was in full swing. The boardwalk running along the front of the bakery was empty. Even the seagulls had given up their patient quest for dropped croissant crumbs. Yellow police tape had been hung haphazardly from one corner of the bakery to the other. It waved wildly in the ocean breeze. It wouldn't be long before it broke free and floated away.

I glanced around briefly, but no one was nearby. Without the lure of pastries and sourdough loaves, people had gone back to their usual morning routines. That was certainly a good thing for my dear friend, Sera. Unfortunately, it also made for a nice motive. While I knew for a fact that Sera and Samuel had no hand in the murder, Norwich would arrest anyone who gave him an easy end to the case.

I ducked under the yellow tape, a rather penetrable barrier. That was not the case with the front door. Much to my surprise and chagrin, Norwich had locked the front door. Or, more likely, his assistant locked it. Norwich was never thorough enough to remember to lock up the crime scene.

Hoping to have luck at the side entrance, I dashed out from under the yellow tape and turned the corner. The clouds and the shade from the museum made the alleyway darker than usual. My foot kicked something small as I reached for the door. It was locked too. I looked around for the object my toe had kicked. Even in the shadow filled alley, it was easy to spot the shiny silver pen. I'd shoved two latex gloves in my pocket in case I found some important evidence. I wasn't entirely sure that was the case with the pen, but I had to be careful. My prints on something near the scene might very well make me the next false arrest.

I turned the pen over on my palm. "Compliments of the Frostfall Hotel," I read. I'd seen the complimentary pens before. The hotel left them in the rooms for guests to use and take home as a souvenir at the end of their stay.

Footsteps landed in the alley. I gasped and spun around and was instantly relieved to see Abner.

"I'm sorry if I startled you, Anna. I was dusting the displays in the main room, and I just happened to glance out the window. I saw you out here."

"That's all right. I was just looking for evidence."

"Oh, so you saw it too," Abner said.

I held up the pen. "Yes, it's from the hotel."

Abner's forehead wrinkled in confusion. "A pen? I wonder how that got here. I was talking about the door lock. It's a little hard to see now that the clouds have blotted out the sun, but it looks as if someone has been tampering with it and I think I know who."

I pulled out my phone and turned on the flashlight. The lock was on a lever style handle. It had been painted white like the door. Abner was right. Some of the white paint had been scratched off around the keyhole as if someone had been trying to poke it with something sharp or possibly even the key itself.

"Are you sure that's not just from Quentin being clumsy with the tip of the key?" I asked.

Abner smiled as if he was the cat that had caught the mouse. "That's what I would have concluded as well if I hadn't caught the culprit red handed. Like I said, I've been doing some dusting. Business at the museum is slow today, so I decided to get in some cleaning to prepare for the summer crowds. I was polishing the large oak captain's wheel with my dust cloth, and I happened to glance out the window. Just like a few minutes ago when I looked out and saw you. Only at that time, I saw a man hunched over the lock. I knew it wasn't Norwich or a police officer, so I walked over and tapped on the window. I scared him. He straightened quickly, and without thinking, he turned my direction." Abner paused for dramatic effect. It was apparent he was enjoying helping out with the murder investigation. In the summer, he told exciting stories about pirate adventures. He was using some of those same storytelling skills now. "It was *him*," he said with a cool, calm seriousness that almost made me laugh.

"Who?" I asked.

"The sourdough man. I won't forget the look of horror on his face when he realized he'd been caught in the act of breaking into the bakery. I hadn't noticed this when he came to the museum that day, but he has a dark birthmark on the right side of his face, in front of his ear."

I practically jumped forward and hugged Abner, but I knew he wasn't the hugging type. "Abner, you're brilliant."

A grin formed on his face. "Do you think we've caught our killer? It seemed he'd returned to the scene of the crime."

"That's because he didn't get his sourdough starter when he killed Quentin. He came back for it."

Abner's thin brows arched. "That makes so much sense. But why didn't he just take it when he came the first time?"

"The only thing I can think of is he panicked and ran."

Abner straightened the sweater vest he was wearing with a sharp, confident tug. "I guess I've had quite the hand in this murder case."

"You've been a great help. Of course, I don't have any proof yet. However, what you witnessed was certainly evidence. My biggest problem now is finding the man. I still don't even know his name, and I can hardly go around asking people if they've seen the sourdough man."

"Gosh, I wish I'd thought to ask him his name when he came to the museum. I often introduce myself and ask people their names, but I was distracted with my paperwork."

I held up the silver pen. "That's all right. I think I might know where to find him, and since he's a stranger on the island, it makes perfect sense."

Abner glanced at the pen in my hand. "That's one of the Frostfall Hotel souvenir pens. I find them all the time on the boardwalk and in the museum. Do you think he dropped it when I startled him?"

"That could very well be, in which case I owe you another

thanks. You said he has a birthmark on the right side of his face. Anything else you can remember? Every little bit helps."

Abner rubbed his chin in thought. "It all happened so fast. I'm surprised I noticed the birthmark."

I patted his arm. "That's all right. You've given me plenty to work with."

We headed out of the alley. It was much brighter once we were out from the shadows of the buildings, but the sky was still a gloomy gray. The water was choppy, which meant my mom had a rough trip back to the mainland. I would be hearing about that, I was sure.

"I'll bet that Norwich hasn't even started looking for the sourdough man." He laughed. "You're right. That is not a proper name for a murder suspect." His smile faded. "But, Anna, you shouldn't be following the man if he's dangerous. We both saw what he did to Quentin." Abner's face blanched a little as the kitchen scene came back to him.

"Don't worry, Abner. I'll be careful. And thanks again for all your help with this case."

His grin returned. "My pleasure and anytime."

twenty-nine

I WORKED on a plan as I headed toward the Frostfall Hotel. The hotel was a large historical building with a red roof and charming rooms that looked out over the harbor. You had to book a room, especially one with a view, well in advance during the summer months. It was much easier to reserve a room during the other seasons unless the island was hosting an event. But there were no events on the calendar. It made sense that the sourdough man was staying at the hotel. There were a few other rentals and camping spots on the island. Otherwise, the hotel was your only option for an overnight stay.

The sun was finally managing to poke its long, glowing arms through a few chinks in the cloudy armor. I still had my sweatshirt zipped up tight. My cheeks felt chapped from the cold, salty air as I hurried along the boardwalk. I had no real plan on how to find my suspect or what I would do if I ran into him. Abner was right. With the way Quentin died, the sourdough man should be considered dangerous. Even if he wasn't armed. It almost made someone more dangerous if they could bludgeon someone to death with a heavy object. And that thought made me stop in the middle of the boardwalk.

"The heavy object?" I glanced back to make sure no bikes were coming before crossing over to one of the many benches along the boardwalk. Two pigeons were, at first, curious about me. They cocked their small heads as their claws gripped the top of the bench. Do you happen to have a pocket full of bread crumbs, they seemed to be saying. When they realized I was only there for a phone call, they fluttered off with an irritated cooing sound.

I'd been so busy, I'd forgotten to call my one good source at the city police precinct. Mindy used to be an island local. She moved to the mainland and got a job in police dispatch. Now she worked at an administrative desk in the precinct. She was always in the know about what was happening in the station, including when Norwich had to travel to Frostfall for a case. She picked up after three rings. "I was wondering when I'd hear from my good friend, Anna."

"Hello, my friend, how are things going on the big island?" Back when she'd made the decision to leave Frostfall, she assured all of us she was just moving to a much bigger island, namely the entire North American continent. Technically, she wasn't wrong.

"Everything is great here, but I've heard you Frostfallians have had another mishap."

I laughed. "I like that name for our kind. It fits. Yes, as

you've heard, there's been a murder, and we've been blessed with the presence of a certain toothpick-gnawing detective."

Mindy giggled. "Oh my gosh, I forgot to tell you—" She lowered her voice. I could picture her hunched in her little cubicle, glancing around to make sure no one was near. "Norwich showed up to a meeting with the captain with that darn toothpick hanging from his mouth. The captain told him if he ever walked into his office with that toothpick again, he was going to make Norwich eat the darn thing."

I had a good snicker. Anytime Norwich was having a bad day was a good day in my book. "I wish I could have been a fly on the wall."

"That job fell to Erica, the captain's administrative assistant. She was in the meeting waiting to take notes. The captain told her to write down what he'd told Norwich, so it would be official. Erica and I went to lunch that day. She told me all about it. It's all hush-hush, of course, because she's not supposed to talk about anything from the meetings. She couldn't keep that good morsel secret." Mindy giggled again. "She said she thought Norwich was going to suck that toothpick right down his throat after the captain made the threat."

"He was still chewing a toothpick when he arrived at the murder scene," I said.

"I think he waits until he leaves the precinct, then he sticks it in. I'm just as happy not to see those spitty toothpicks dangling from his lip. He sometimes comes to my cubicle and hangs over me with that creepy expression he considers a smile. I always lean back, afraid spittle will fly when he talks. Anyhow, enough about that. It's turning my stomach talking about the man."

"I'm with you there. Did you happen to get a look at the coroner's report for Quentin Oxley?"

"Sure did. I had to scan the report into the file. Who was Quentin Oxley? The name is not familiar."

"He was fairly new to the island. He was a French trained pastry chef who took the island by storm with his chocolate croissants and sugary pastries."

"Ahh, what a shame. I can see where a bakery would be a big hit on Frostfall."

"Yes, but these croissants came with a great deal of controversy. Quentin was rude, arrogant and he didn't seem to care whose feelings he hurt."

The background noise at the station was always a discordant mix of sounds. This morning was no different. "So, he was asking for it," Mindy said.

"I don't know if anyone deserves what he got, no matter how unpleasant, but when you make enemies, you have to expect problems."

"Hold on, I've got another call." Mindy moved to the other call and came right back. "They're on hold so I'll hurry. It looks like the victim died from a crushed skull. There were two blows to his head with a heavy object."

"Does the coroner say anything more specific about the object?"

She paused. "The lesser of the two blows showed bruising on his scalp. It seemed the weapon had a row of small squares. Could it have been a meat tenderizer? Those are heavy, and they have rows of squares."

"That's true, Mindy. I hadn't thought of that."

"So you knew about the row of squares?"

"Sort of. But I'll let you get to your other call. As usual, my friend, you were a big help. And the toothpick story has made my day." I hung up and stood from the bench wearing a big smile. That disappeared instantly when I spotted the toothpick chewer himself strutting down the boardwalk. One uniformed officer accompanied him.

I waited to see which way he turned. A right turn might indicate that he was heading toward Jack's restaurant. A left would mean he was heading in the direction of Sera's tea shop. It seemed Jack was going to win the day's terrible contest. It also meant that there was no way I could avoid running into Norwich unless I ducked behind Molly's produce stand. I decided to just face him. With any luck, I could fill his head with doubt about a possible arrest of Jack Drake.

His sneer was one of the ugliest sneers on the planet, and I didn't even need to see everyone else's sneers to know that. "St. James, what are you doing out here?"

I held up my arms and looked around. "You mean out on the island where I live?"

Norwich didn't even try to hide his suspicious scowl. "All I know is that you're always nosing around in places you shouldn't be." He glanced in the direction of the bakery. "You better not be contaminating my crime scene. Otherwise, I'll haul you in for murder. It'll just take one fingerprint connecting you to Oxley's death, and you'll be baking cookies behind bars."

I tilted my head and forced a smile. "I didn't realize they let people bake in prison." I looked at the young officer for confirmation. He wore the same mystified, horrified and confused look of any rookie officer who was unlucky enough to get chosen for the job of assisting Norwich.

"Just stay out of my way, St. James," Norwich growled around his toothpick.

"Gladly." This time I looked in the direction of the bakery. "You aren't here for an arrest, are you? Or did you find the mysterious stranger who's been lurking around the bakery? He was also seen arguing with Oxley the day before the murder. Something about Oxley stealing an heirloom from his family. Oh, but I don't have to tell you all this. I'm sure you're way ahead of me. You probably already have the name and identity of the man." As I spoke, I was sure he'd bite the toothpick in half.

His assistant was looking at him now with even more confusion. "I thought Mr. Drake was an island local?"

My hunch had been right. Norwich was ready to wrongly arrest Jack Drake. I hoped my ploy had stopped him from making another huge mistake, one that would greatly affect my friend.

I decided to add a little icing on top to seal the deal. "In fact, Abner spotted the stranger this morning trying to break into the side door on the bakery. Guess he hadn't found what he was looking for yet. I'm sure Abner can fill you in on the details." I hated to add this to Abner's plate, but it was a better alternative to watching Jack be taken away in handcuffs.

A red flush of anger was rising up along the greasy collar of Norwich's coat. "Of course I know about that suspect." It was a lie, but I smiled and nodded. "I was just heading to talk to Abner right now." He took a few steps. "Where can I find this guy, Abner?"

"Were you planning to just wander the island calling out the name until someone answered?"

The same red flush crept up his face. "St. James," he growled through gritted teeth.

"I was just having some fun. We cookie bakers don't get out enough, I guess. Abner Plunkett runs the museum." I pointed. "The museum is the big white building with the word museum on its sign."

Norwich grumbled something to the officer, and they headed in the direction of the museum. I sent off a quick text to Abner to warn him and then I picked up my pace. Unfortunately, I still had no idea how I was going to find the sourdough man. I was really starting to like that nickname. Too bad the guy was a killer.

thirty

IT WAS RELATIVELY quiet in the vast lobby of the hotel. It was only Thursday, and weekenders didn't usually check in until Friday. I circled the main sitting area where people waited for the ferry or for a friend to join them. Only one elderly woman sat on the tufted, emerald green velvet couches. She held onto her cane with one hand and clutched a paperback novel in the other. I walked down the hallway past the various conference rooms. A sign outside one announced that it would be the meeting place for the Country Botanical Society. Staff members were busy vacuuming and setting up tables. There was no sign of my suspect. I wasn't entirely sure if I'd recognize him. I'd only seen him in the shadows and briefly as he brushed past me from the bakery alley. Abner's mention of the dark birthmark on his face would certainly help. Not many people had birthmarks on their face and, specifically, in front of their right ear. I still had no idea what I would say to the man, but that didn't stop me from forging ahead with my search.

I headed back across the lobby and over to the hotel restaurant. It was a popular eating place on the island, even for locals. There was an outdoor patio with tables and heating lamps for cold weather. A young woman named Phoenix, a name I always remembered because it was so unusual, was the hostess for the restaurant. Phoenix lived with her grandparents down near the swimming beach.

"Hello, Anna." She picked up a menu. "Would you like to eat inside or out?"

"Actually, I'm here looking for a friend. Would you mind if I walked around the dining area?"

"Not at all. Don't forget to check the outside tables." She was sweet and I hated to lie, but sometimes an investigation with no badge to back it up required *creative* thinking. One thing I quickly discovered was that it was hard to look inconspicuous when you were searching a dining room for a certain face and a specific birthmark. I swept my eyes from table to table as I strolled casually down each aisle. Only half the tables were occupied, which helped my mission. I couldn't imagine trying to do the same thing during a busy summer lunch hour. There was no sign of the man with the birthmark. I'd switched to mentally calling him that because sourdough man wasn't fitting with the mental image of my very serious murder investigation.

I pushed through the glass door that took me to the outdoor tables. Only two tables were occupied, one a couple with two small children and the other the elderly woman with the book and cane. It seemed her friend had arrived for their lunch. The heating lamps were putting off a luxurious warmth that countered the cold breeze coming off the water.

I headed back in through the dining area, took one more glance around and walked back out.

"No luck?" Phoenix asked.

"No, we must have gotten our signals crossed." That was the other problem with lying. You had to keep at it to continue the ruse.

"Don't forget, there's a patio area on the roof. Some people take their lunches to go, so they can sit up there. It's not a great day for it, but the view is still amazing."

"Right, the rooftop patio. I'd forgotten all about that. Thanks." My steps were far more plodding than when I first arrived. I was starting to get that sinking feeling that my suspect was no longer at the hotel. Still, Frannie would have let me know if he'd left the island. There was always the possibility that he'd arrived on a private boat. But Abner had seen him this morning, and it seemed he still hadn't gotten hold of his sourdough starter.

I stepped into the elevator and hit the button for the top floor. A staircase at the end of the hallway led up to the rooftop patio. I'd only been up there a few times, but I knew Phoenix was right. The view was amazing. On a clear day, you could see all the way to the high rises in the city. Thinking of the city reminded me that I needed to check that Mom got home all right. I'd text her on my way back down.

I stepped into the long hallway. Lush carpeting ran the length of the rooms. Several room service trays sat outside of doors. There was always the possibility that my suspect was still holed up in his room enjoying room service. Maybe Abner had scared him off for good, and he'd given up the quest for the sourdough. Would someone give up that easily after they'd murdered for it? I knew one thing for certain. Norwich was not anywhere near closing in on the man. Was I?

The rooftop patio was deserted. It made sense because there were no heat lamps, and it was far too cold and breezy to sit on top of the hotel. The few rays of sunlight had vanished too.

I headed quickly back inside. My sweatshirt was no match for the rooftop weather. I got back into the elevator and pulled out my phone. I leaned against the railing on the back wall and texted my mom. "Just checking that you got in all right."

The elevator stopped at a middle floor as she texted back. "I'm here, but I sure wish I'd gotten Cora to come back with me."

A new passenger stepped into the elevator.

I texted back a sad face emoji and put my phone back in my pocket. As I looked up, the man who'd entered turned his face slightly to the side. The breath stuck in my chest. He had a birthmark. It was *the* birthmark. It was sourdough man. I'd switched back to that name because somehow it made him seem less menacing, like the Pillsbury Doughboy.

We reached the lobby. My heart was racing as fast as my mind. At least we were no longer inside an elevator. I followed him across the lobby. He paused and looked back, seemingly thinking he was being followed. Which he was. I didn't know how to be stealthier in the middle of a hotel lobby.

I needed to act fast before he walked out and I had to chase him down the boardwalk. Inside the lobby, I felt pretty certain he wouldn't pull out his meat tenderizer and clobber me on the skull.

He stopped to read the menu posted outside the restaurant. I cleared my throat loudly. "Did you get back your sourdough starter?" I asked.

His face snapped my direction. "Excuse me?"

"I saw you arguing with the baker, Quentin Oxley. You were trying to get him to return your sourdough starter. I sure wouldn't want anything to happen to mine. I've had it for five years."

He nodded. "Mine is over a hundred years old, and no, I haven't gotten it back." He squinted with suspicion as he turned toward me. One hand was in his coat pocket. The pocket didn't look big enough for a meat tenderizer. "Why are you asking?"

Before I could come up with a response, he jumped in again.

"I didn't kill him, if that's what you were thinking."

"What? No, of course not. Why would I think that?" We were standing in a very public place, which gave me a spurt of courage I wouldn't have had in the elevator. "All right. Maybe it crossed my mind. I saw you early one morning near the bakery. Someone else spotted you earlier today at the side door of the bakery. I'm Anna, by the way." It was funny, but something about the man's face, birthmark and all, made me feel at ease. I wasn't standing toe to toe with a killer, just a man determined to get back his family's heirloom. Unless I was entirely wrong and my usual sense about these things had been thrown off by the chaotic start to the week.

"I'm Terry. I was at the bakery door today hoping I could get in—"

"You mean break in?"

He glanced down with a touch of shame. It further solidified my first instincts about the man. How could I have been so convinced he was the killer? My intuition was usually better than that. Was I subconsciously ready to pounce on a suspect because I wanted to clear the names of my friends? Still, he had some explaining to do.

"It's true, I was trying to pick the lock, but only because I'm that desperate to find that sourdough starter." Another glance down and this one with a slight flush of his cheeks. "I promised my parents I'd get it back. We own a bakery in Boston. Our sourdough bread is our claim to fame. Quentin interned with us when he was fresh out of pastry school. He was difficult and arrogant, but my parents kept him on. They even let him rent the apartment above the bakery for almost nothing. Then he betrayed them. He packed up one night and left… with the starter. My father was devastated. It was from his great-grandmother. Now that Quentin is dead, and the bakery is locked up, I fear I won't be able to get the starter. I can't go home without it. Like I said, I promised my parents."

I was feeling a sharp pang of guilt. I'd set Norwich on Terry's trail, insinuating that he was the killer. I'd done it to protect Jack's reputation. He was right. Even if he was innocent and immediately released, the shocking spectacle of him being taken away in handcuffs would last forever.

"I'm sorry for asking, but the homicide detective is on the island, and I'm worried he'll arrest the wrong person. He has a tendency to do just that. Were you at the bakery that morning hoping you could approach Quentin about the sourdough?"

"I already knew he wasn't going to hand it over. I was prepared to confront him and make some legal threats. I just couldn't work up the nerve. The guy was mean and despicable and—I know it's not nice to say stuff like that about him since he's dead but—"

"But he *was* mean and despicable. I witnessed him at his worst several times. He managed to make a lot of enemies on this island."

Terry grinned lightly. "I guess sometimes people do get what they deserve." He rolled his lips in and blushed again. "I'm sorry, that was a terrible thing to say."

"It's all right. I understand."

Terry snapped his fingers. "That morning, when I was standing outside the bakery hoping to work up the courage to confront Quentin, someone else was there. A man. He was pounding angrily on the front door, but Quentin wouldn't open."

"Yes, you're right." I'd been so focused on the sourdough man, I'd forgotten all about Jamie Baxter's confrontation with the victim. And Murray Hogan, Sally's husband, had approached Quentin too. I had their names on my corkboards, but I'd spent all my time chasing down this lead. I knew why. I preferred to have the killer be someone who wasn't a friend or acquaintance or, for that matter, a local.

"How did he die?" Terry asked.

"Blow to the head." There was no reason to add in gory details. I'd been wasting my time. If Terry was the killer, he was putting on the most brilliant poker face of all time. He just didn't have murderer in his expression. For the past few days, he'd been a shadowy figure lurking around with seemingly nefarious intentions. Now that I'd spoken to my sourdough man, he had a face, a kind one at that and he seemed to be genuinely only interested in taking back what rightfully belonged to him.

Terry's eyes rounded. Something seemed to click again. "Now that I think about it, I saw the same man, the big one with the red hair who'd pounded on the bakery door, that same night. I'd returned to the bakery hoping to talk to Quentin again. I'd had a couple of beers at the hotel bar, and I talked myself into going over there. I was desperate and unsure of how to proceed. All I knew was my parents were waiting for me to return with the starter. Anyhow, I was too late. Quentin had locked up, and the bakery was dark. As I reached the bakery, the red haired man was marching past, fists rolled up and growling under his breath."

I nodded. "Interesting." I wasn't about to let him know that I knew the man with the red hair just in case he was using Jamie as a decoy. If it was true, then I needed to take a serious look at Jamie Baxter. He had motive. Remi didn't try to hide the fact that she was sweet on the new baker, and jealousy could push people over the edge. "Thanks for talking to me. Are you staying on the island for much longer? Maybe I can figure out a way to get you into that bakery for your sourdough," I added quickly.

"I'll be here two more days. I sure would appreciate if you could help me with that." He handed me a business card for the Boule Bakery in Boston. "That's my cell phone on the bottom."

I pocketed the card. I doubted a killer would hand out a business card with a name and phone number. I was going to have to focus on a new suspect. I'd hoped to have this wrapped up quickly, to save Jack the agony of waiting and wondering, but I had more sleuthing to do. The only person at home for lunch was Opal, and she never minded making herself a sandwich. I'd head home and grab my bicycle. I needed some wheels to get around faster. It was time to focus on some of the other suspects on the corkboard.

thirty-one

IT HAD ALREADY BEEN a long day, so I made myself sit down and eat a piece of toast with tea as I scanned my colorful corkboards. There were so many suspects on the boards, but after this morning's interaction, the sourdough man had moved down the list. It was sad to realize that Jamie had moved up to the top. I needed to talk to him. I hoped I was wrong. Then there was Murray Hogan and his wife Sally. She had worked hard for Quentin only to be told she wasn't doing a good enough job. He must have really pushed all her buttons to get her to quit. But had he pushed the last one, the one that motivated her to kill him? Sally didn't seem a likely suspect for murder, particularly one that took some strength and a lot of anger. Murray, on the other hand, was a big, sturdy guy. He looked plenty mad the morning I saw him walking away from the bakery.

I'd had no text or SOS signal from Jack, so I assumed my

little talk with Norwich had sent him on a new chase. I felt confident he wouldn't find Terry. Norwich ran such a surface-only investigation; he'd never track down the mystery man.

I finished my snack and hurried out to my bicycle. The earlier clouds had been sifted into feathery wisps of white allowing for much more sunlight. I hopped on my bike and pedaled toward the harbor. Most of the fishermen would be back in their slips getting their boats ready for the next day's catch. I was sure I'd find Jamie working on his boat. I didn't look forward to the awkward conversation we were about to have.

As I neared the row of fishing trawlers moored along the docks, I caught sight of a yellow rain slicker stretched over broad shoulders. It was Jamie. The early morning clouds had most likely meant a drippy, dreary day out on the water. The rain slicker made sense. It also triggered a memory. Occasionally, snippets of my short married life with Michael resurfaced. I was sure the unsettling photo bomber in our wedding picture had brought them all bubbling to the top. All it took was the yellow rubber Mackintosh to take me back in time. I stopped pedaling and put my feet down to catch my breath. I was supposed to be figuring out what to say to Jamie. Instead, a clear memory stormed through my mind. It happened just a month before Michael disappeared. Up until now, I'd repressed it under the layers of good memories I was working hard to hold onto. But this wasn't one of those. This one had left me feeling hurt and somewhat baffled.

I folded the tuna sandwiches up into parchment paper and placed them in the lunch cooler next to the stack of oatmeal cookies. Huck was waiting anxiously by the door. The dog knew parchment wrapped sandwiches and the cooler meant a walk to the marina to see Michael. Some of Huck's enthusiasm might have been due to the small extra sandwich I'd packed for him.

Michael spent a good two hours on his boat *Wild Rose* after he'd dropped his catch at the fish market across the harbor. Every once in awhile, I liked to surprise him by bringing lunch down to the boat. We'd eat sandwiches, and Michael would tell me about his day on the water. I'd made a batch of oatmeal cookies, his favorite and by the time they were out of the oven, I'd made a plan to take him lunch.

It was a brisk, beautiful day on the island. The kind that made me marvel at how lucky I'd gotten marrying the man I loved and living on a piece of paradise. I never looked back to my life and career in the city. Frostfall was my home now, and I had no plans to ever leave it.

Huck bounded ahead. He knew exactly where we were going and would reach the boat long before my feet caught up to him. It would ruin the surprise, but I didn't mind. The oatmeal cookies and lunch with his adoring wife were the real surprises.

I'd just crossed the boardwalk to the docks when Huck came trotting back. He looked a little forlorn until he saw that I still carried the lunch cooler and his treat. He sniffed the pail and wagged his tail.

"Why are you back, Huck?" I shaded my eyes and looked down the line of fishing boats being prepped for tomorrow's catch. Michael's slip was empty. The *Wild Rose* hadn't returned. For a short, few seconds, I managed to push myself into a full panic, worried something had happened. Huck's bark whipped me out of my thoughts, and my gaze lifted to the harbor. The familiar chug of the *Rose's* motor made me sigh with relief. I glanced at my watch. He was over an hour late.

Huck and I waited patiently at the slip and helped tie off the boat. Michael looked decidedly grumpy with a scowl that could compete with Ebenezer Scrooge for meanest face. I smiled up at him as he put his hand out to help me on board, but he didn't look at me. Huck hopped on deck. Michael grumbled angrily about his muddy paws. This surprise lunch wasn't going at all like I thought.

I held up the cooler. "I brought tuna sandwiches and a surprise."

He said nothing but turned back to his pile of nets. The deck still smelled strongly of fish. Silver scales dotted the worn, wet teak planks. "Did you have a bad catch?" Lately the catches had been low. I knew he was worried about his income.

"It was fine," he said curtly.

"Why were you so late? Engine trouble?" There I was, curious Anna trying hard to find out why he was in such a bad mood. His late return to the island had to have something to do with it.

"I'm not late. I just stayed on shore longer than usual. Can you grab the mop and start cleaning the deck?"

"Sure," I said with little enthusiasm. I placed the lunch cooler inside the wheelhouse and pulled the mop out of the storage closet. I wasn't wearing proper shoes for mopping the deck. I had to concentrate on where I placed my feet or risk slipping on a plank that had been worn smooth from many footsteps.

An insatiable curiosity prodded me to ask more questions. "What were you doing on shore for so long?"

"Anna," he said sharply. "Just pay attention. You're missing too many spots." And that seemed to be the only answer I would get. I wanted to take the lunch cooler, cookies and all, and toss them into the ocean. The lunch surprise was a disaster. His tone had stung so much, I tossed aside the mop.

"Huck, let's go," I said. Huck bounded off the boat. I wasn't able to make quite so quick and elegant of an exit. It would have gone better with my dramatic storm off.

"Anna, wait, I'm sorry," Michael said as my feet finally landed on the dock. I didn't look back.

"Anna," a familiar voice called through the fog of my daydream. "Everything all right?" Frannie asked. She was eating lunch on the bench at the ferry dock.

I waved and smiled. "Everything is fine." I didn't have

time for a chat. I needed to catch Jamie before he left the boat. I took a deep breath, whisking away the heavy feeling the memory had left me with. I climbed off my bike and walked it toward the fishing boats.

thirty-two

JAMIE BAXTER WAS FINISHING up in his wheelhouse when I reached the boat. I leaned my bike against a pylon and waved at him. He waved back through the water spotted glass. "Hello, Anna, what brings you out here?" he said as he stepped down from his wheelhouse.

"Actually, Jamie, I was hoping to talk to you about something important."

"Sure," he said tentatively. Jamie had thick red hair and the freckles that went along with being a true ginger. Unlike the fiery red on Opal's head, which could take on many shades of color depending on how long it had been since she'd dyed it.

His big work boots pounded the planks as he stepped off the boat onto the dock. He towered over me. I smiled up at him sheepishly. "I've forgotten how tall you are. I do remember you always needing three sandwiches whenever you went out on the boat with Michael." I figured a little reminiscing and reminding him that Michael gave him his start in the fishing industry would soften him up.

"You do make terrific sandwiches." He pulled a rag from the pocket of his raincoat and wiped his hands. "What's this about, Anna?"

"I'm sure you heard that Frostfall's newest resident was killed in his bakery."

"Might have heard something." His face suddenly looked less friendly, and he concentrated more on wiping his hands, even though there was nothing left to wipe. He finally put away the rag and looked at me. "I know you're probably out investigating the crime, but you've come to the wrong guy. Yeah, I was mad as a rabid dog at that jerk. Who did he think he was coming onto my island and stealing my girl?" The topic was bringing up the same ire I'd witnessed outside the bakery that morning. "I didn't kill him, Anna. You've got to believe me. In fact, I'm all through with Remi. I told her she could keep him. I've been talking with this sweet woman at the fish market. We're going on a date next weekend."

"I'm glad you're over the heartbreak already. How is Remi?"

Jamie laughed. "I imagine she's having all sorts of regrets. Oxley wasn't all that interested. She wrecked a good thing between us. I was planning on proposing this summer. She begged me to take her back, but I told her we were through."

His words reminded me that Frannie had witnessed a scene where it seemed Remi was pleading with Jamie. Now I knew for certain what it was about. Remi had broken off with

Jamie to be with Quentin, only Quentin just as quickly brushed her off.

"I'm sorry this happened. You two made such a nice couple," I said.

"We did, and that's what I told her, but she thought that guy Oxley was going to be her Prince Charming. I guess he really poured it on at first, promising her trips to Paris and all that but then he just as quickly lost interest. I haven't talked to Remi since yesterday when she came out here to beg me to take her back. She left here crying her eyes out. I guess you lie in the bed you make."

"I do feel bad for the both of you. Jamie, I've got to ask— where were you yesterday morning between the hours of four and seven?"

Jamie chuckled. "And you the wife of a fisherman. I was right here on this rusty tin bucket getting ready to head out for the morning. You can ask Hector." He motioned with his head to the next boat. "We had a cup of coffee together about half-past four. I was spilling my guts to him, so I'm sure he'll remember it. Not going to spill any more guts over Remi Seymour. I was ready to make her my wife. We'd talked about our future together many times, but you can't marry someone you don't trust." His words felt a little haunting after the terrible day on the *Wild Rose*. I'd never found out what Michael was up to that day. I brought it up once more. He answered just as sharply, so I never asked again.

"I won't keep you, Jamie. I know you're busy. Thanks for talking to me, and again, I'm sorry about the breakup."

thirty-three

I WAS AT A LOSS. Jamie had good motive, but he had a solid alibi. I didn't need to ask Hector about the cup of coffee. I trusted Jamie. I'd known him since he was in his early twenties. He was always kind and likeable and responsible. He handled the breakup maturely. Jamie had come to the conclusion that he couldn't count on Remi's love. Someone else came along offering more adventure or travel or whatever Quentin had promised, and Remi didn't think twice about breaking Jamie's heart. I was sure it was the hardest thing he'd ever done, not taking her back. In time, with wounds healed, maybe they'd find each other again. But this would at least show Remi that she couldn't take Jamie's love for granted. And I was telling myself all this mostly because I was grappling with two pulls on my heart strings. The first one was something I couldn't understand—the unexplained presence of Michael's high school sweetheart at our wedding. Then there was that everlasting worry I felt about Nate getting tired of island life and moving back to the city to start over. The second one felt fresher, more raw because, even if I didn't say it out loud, I'd fallen in love with Nate. The first one was bothering me more and more though, and while my brain percolated next steps in the murder investigation, I sat on a bench and pulled out my phone. Fortunately, Denise Fengarten was not a common name. It was entirely possible she had a different last name now, but information and a phone number for a Denise Fengarten in Rhode Island popped to the top of the search list.

My heart pounded enough that I could feel it against the back of the bench as I typed in the phone number. What would I ask her? Would she be angry I called? Actually, I didn't care if she was. I needed to know why she was at my wedding. She was clearly not invited. The number went instantly to a 'no longer in service' message. My shoulders drooped in a twisted mix of relief and disappointment. Michael was gone. Maybe it was better that I didn't know. As I sat there working hard to push uncomfortable thoughts out of my mind, Murray and Sally Hogan strolled past on the boardwalk. They were holding hands and smiling. They were two people on my corkboards that I hadn't seen since the murder. I got up from the bench and hurried to catch up to them.

"You two look happy. Are you heading to Jack's place?'

Murray looked back first. They stopped. "Anna, good to see you. We both had a hankering for some of that good Pirate's Gold fried chicken."

Sally placed her hand on my arm. "I'm sure you heard about Quentin. Horrible thing."

"Of course, she's heard about it." Murray pulled his hat down lower. The breeze coming off the harbor was sharper than usual. "She's going to find the killer. Isn't that right, Anna?"

They were such a sweet couple I wasn't sure how to work my way around to questioning them. If I was too blunt, they might not speak to me again, and on such a small island that wasn't easy. There was no way to avoid each other.

"I hope I can find who did this," I said. The gears were spinning. How to approach this with discretion? Sally and Murray had no idea they were on my corkboards. I intended on keeping it that way. At the same time, I couldn't check them off entirely. They had motive, and Murray had made it clear that Quentin angered him a great deal. "Sally, I heard you quit the bakery job."

Sally's mouth puckered a little. She fidgeted with the edges of her sweater. "It was a mutual decision. It wasn't working out, so we both agreed I should leave. Quentin wanted me to stay until he found a replacement, but I told him I wanted nothing more to do with his bakery."

"Good riddance too. That job was making her so stressed, she couldn't sleep or eat. I had more than a few words with that Oxley about how he was treating her."

Sally squeezed his arm and looked up at him with a smile. "You've always been my knight in shining armor." As I stood there talking to them, I easily convinced myself they were not killers.

"Maybe you can help me, Sally. When was the last time you saw Quentin?"

Sally looked a little surprised but not taken aback by the question. "Why, I guess it was Tuesday afternoon, my last work shift. I admit, I was crying as I left the bakery. It upset me because I felt as if I'd failed at my job."

Murray put his arm around her shoulder. "You weren't the failure, Sally, my peach. It was that awful man. I can't say I'm sorry or surprised that he's dead. He was the most abrasive person I've ever had the misfortune to meet. I won't lie. I almost hit him. When I went to talk to him about the way he was treating my Sally, I had my fists tight as iron balls. Still wish I'd given him a good one. Would have made me feel better."

Sally rolled her eyes. "It also would have had you arrested for assault. Besides, none of that matters now." She focused back on me. "Anna, who do you think did it?" She laughed. "I heard some outlandish rumors that Detective Norwich was going to arrest Jack Drake for the murder. Have you ever heard anything so ridiculous?"

Murray looked down at her. "But, Sal, you told me Jack and Quentin were always fighting, something about the smells from Jack's seafood ruining the pastries."

"It's true." Sally crinkled her nose. "Sometimes, when Jack was cooking shrimp or fish, the odors would seep into the bakery, mostly from people going in and out of the door. It made the bakery treats a little less enticing. But it didn't hurt business, so I don't know why Quentin put up such a fuss. He threatened Jack with all kinds of stuff, health inspectors, lawsuits." Sally gasped and her eyes rounded. "My gosh, you don't think it was Jack, do you?"

"No, we all know Jack. He's not a killer," I assured her.

"Well, I hope you find the person soon. None of us are safe with a killer running around the island," Murray said.

"I'm working on it. Enjoy your lunch." As I spun around, I nearly ran into two women walking bicycles over to the bike racks. "Oops, excuse me," I said and continued to my own bike that was still resting against the back of the bench. I walked my bike around to the boardwalk. I needed to get dinner prepped, and I was officially stalled on the case. I'd promised to find the killer soon so Jack could rest easy, and so far, I'd failed.

As I rolled my bike past the two women, something caught my eye. One of the women was snapping shut her bike lock. It had a solid cylinder with a line of squares. Each square had a number, the numbers used to open the lock. It wasn't the first time I'd seen that style of bike lock. I quickly took out my phone and pulled up the photo of the bread dough in Quentin's hand. The imprint looked very much like the bike lock.

I hopped on my bike. Dinner would have to wait. I needed to talk to Remi Seymour.

thirty-four

REMI SEYMOUR RENTED a small cottage near the swimming beach. I'd been there once, about a year ago, when she invited me over to talk about a job at the financial firm she worked at. They had an opening for a remote position, like hers. I gave it about ten minutes thought before reminding myself that I wasn't looking to get back into the business world.

The cold air chapped my cheeks and made my eyes burn as I pedaled through the quiet neighborhoods bordering the swim beach. Remi's rental was not on the beach. Those locations were for the million dollar houses, but it was just three blocks and a short walk from the path leading down to the sand. It was a great location, and her cottage looked cozy. A wind chime made of seashells fluttered in the breeze producing a charming sound. Two wicker chairs and a matching wicker table were set up on the front porch. A magazine sat on the table, its pages whipping back and forth in the wind. Before I climbed the porch steps, I spotted the rear wheel of a bicycle. Presumably, the rest of the bike was hidden behind the privet shrub that ran along that side of the house.

I ducked down to avoid being seen through the window and walked around the corner to get a better look at the bike. I'd seen Remi earlier in the week locking up her bike near the produce stand. I was almost a hundred percent certain that Remi had been using the same style lock that I'd just seen the other cyclist use near the boardwalk bench. But today, there was a different lock on Remi's bike. It was one of the vintage types, a thick chain hidden in a sleeve of unwieldy plastic and a regular padlock holding together the two ends. The chain looked rusty, and there were breaks in the plastic. This bike lock had seen better days.

"Hello?" a voice startled me.

Remi was standing with her arms crossed defensively. "Anna," she said coldly. "Why on earth are you snooping around my house?"

She'd surprised me. I didn't have time to think up a good excuse, so I went with the truth. "I was just checking out your bike lock."

Remi looked down to the end of her driveway where my bicycle was leaning against her mailbox. "Why are you looking at my bike lock?" She asked, and rightly so. Her dark brow arched, and she tightened her arms even more defensively. She sensed something was up. Her reaction to my mention of the bike lock only solidified my latest theory on the murder.

"I thought I saw you with one of those fancy new locks, the kind that have the row of numbers. I wanted to get something like that for my bike. But I see you have one of those big heavy chain locks like I used to have when I was a kid."

"That's right. Those are the most reliable." She seemed to be telling herself to stop acting so suspicious. She lowered her arms and smiled, but it was a hard smile that nearly cracked her face. "Guess the stuff they made during those boomer years was sometimes better."

"First of all, I'm not a boomer." I shook my head, angry that I let that comment get to me when I had a much more important matter at hand. "It's just that I'm sure I saw you with one of those new locks earlier this week. I was buying produce, and you were locking it up across from the produce stand."

"Nope," she said curtly. "Maybe you need some glasses." She turned to go back inside.

"One of those new bike locks was used to kill Quentin Oxley." I blurted it out. That stopped her cold in her tracks.

She spun back around. "How can you possibly know that?" She laughed dryly. "That's right. You consider yourself some sort of detective. This place is laughable. It's so hokey. I can't wait to move away from here. Then I never have to see Frostfall or any of its inhabitants again."

"Inhabitants like the man you cheated on with Quentin Oxley? I'm just glad Jamie's moved on. I suppose it was all worth it until Quentin told you he was no longer interested. You gave up a good thing, a sure thing, a future with a man who adored you and who would see to your every happiness, and all for a man who had no real interest in you at all."

Her face was red with anger. "Not true. Quentin said he loved me."

"It seems like he told you a lot of things, promises of trips to Paris, world travels? Only he was just stringing you along. When he dumped you, it was too late for you and Jamie. He wouldn't take you back."

Remi stomped toward me. I quickly reminded myself about the violent scene I'd found inside the bakery. If Remi was the killer, and I had everything but an actual confession assuring me that was the case, then she had a terrible, violent temper.

"You don't know anything."

"I know you used your other bike lock to kill Quentin. Only, one blow didn't do it. You had to hit him twice." She flinched as I spoke. Her upper lip began twitching.

"I wasn't going to kill him. I just wanted to hurt him like he hurt me. After the first blow, he fell down and told me he'd have me arrested and put away forever. So, I hit him again. I knew I had to finish him off. But I'm not going to jail," she said through gritted teeth.

Then she moved so quickly, I didn't see it coming. Her hands shot out, and she slammed me in the stomach. I fell back hard, landing mostly on my tailbone. The air shot out of me. As I struggled to regain my breath, Remi grabbed her bicycle. She whipped her long leg over and pedaled away.

After a few good seconds of pure panic, I was able to take a breath. Pain shot through my back as I sat up and then pushed to my feet. "I'm not getting paid enough for this," I muttered as I trotted clumsily and in pain down the driveway. "That's right. I'm not getting paid at all," I reminded myself as I heaved my leg over my bicycle. Remi disappeared around the corner. She'd had a head start and rode her bike all the time. I wouldn't think about the fact that she was also ten years younger. I already had enough going against me. The one thing I had in my favor was that we lived on an island. There just weren't that many places Remi could go.

thirty-five

"JUST WHAT I NEEDED." A cold drizzle started falling. Twenty minutes earlier the air was cold, but there'd been no rain. A dark layer of clouds turned the sky menacing. It was the kind of sky that, when spotted at sea, made ship captains quiver in fear. On the island, it meant we were going to get a downpour. The drizzle was just the opening act.

The pain in my back had mostly subsided. Take that, you thirty something killer, I thought wryly. I was pedaling faster than I had ever pedaled. At the same time, I regretted that I'd ridden out today without a helmet. In my defense, I'd gone out to ride casually, slowly from location to location. I hadn't expected to be engaged in a high-speed bicycle chase. Remi was still a good half mile ahead of me on Island Drive. It was the only paved road on the entire island, and the mist was making the asphalt slick. As light as the rain was that fell from the gunmetal gray sky, my jeans and sweatshirt were very wet. Even though I was getting one heck of a workout, a shiver was starting deep inside. My chin was beginning to do that thing it did whenever I was truly cold.

This was when it would have come in handy to have some kind of law enforcement on the island. I could have pushed myself up from Remi's front drive, called the police and then pedaled happily home before the cold drizzle had started. Instead, I was chasing a killer around the island. I envisioned us going around and around with no end in sight. I would have loved to ask her exactly what her plan was for escape. Unfortunately, she was too far ahead of me.

The drizzle was making it hard to see. I was going so fast I hardly dared to take my hand off the grip. I did a quick swipe across my eyes to clear them and then hunkered down lower over my handlebars to avoid the icy air that was smacking against me. My biggest worry was that she'd leave the paved road. Her bike was a sturdy mountain bike, the kind Nate and Samuel used for trails in the mountains. My bike was the no-frills cruising type, the kind you put a flowery basket on. Definitely not the kind you take on rough roads.

It seemed Remi had also surmised that my bike wouldn't do too well on a rugged trail. She glanced back once, a wicked smile on her face, before turning sharply onto the small rocky trail that would eventually connect to the bigger, more traveled Calico Trail. The back pain returned as my tires hit the rocky section of trail. My tail-bone smacked the seat, and I had a hard time holding onto the handlebars. The fact that my hands were numb from the cold rain didn't help matters. Twice, I had to jam my foot against a rock to keep from toppling over. I could have moved faster on foot, but I'd need the bike when we reached Calico Trail. After that, there were only two paths to take—toward Calico Peak or around North Pond and back down the other side of the island. I didn't know what Remi was thinking at this point. Murder could make people a little unhinged, and Remi was definitely that. Earlier, I'd felt sorry for her. She'd been badly used by one man and then cast aside by another. But the long, arduous and occasionally treacherous bike ride was making me rethink my earlier moment of sympathy.

I was losing the chase. Her bicycle and, as much as I hated to admit it, her riding skills were so superior there was no way for me to catch up to her. Fortunately, I had the island on my side. If I continued to follow her, eventually, she'd realize there was no place to hide. No place to go except the Atlantic Ocean.

In the meantime, it became more important for me to not break any bones than to catch a killer. The terrain around the north end of the pond was still muddy from snowmelt. After navigating a maze of sharp, jutting rocks, I found my bike tires bogged down in after-winter sludge. Remi's mountain bike tires had left tracks in the same syrupy mud. They were already vanishing by the time I reached the area. Her tires had ripped right though the mud, but mine were sticking to it as if it was filled with glue. I tried to pedal hard a few times, but I was only digging myself deeper. It was sucking the bike tires in like quicksand. I had no choice except to climb off the bike and walk it out of the mire. My shoes and the bottom half of my jeans looked as if they'd been dipped in chocolate by the time I reached the other side of the mud.

My chase had not exactly ended dramatically with the murderer pinned under my bike tire like in an action movie. My best option was to make sure Remi didn't get off the island. Once to the other side, she could take off and truly find a hiding place. I pulled out my phone, one of the few things not covered in mud, thankfully. I texted Fran. "Don't let Remi Seymour leave the island. I'll explain later."

She wrote back seconds later. "This, I can't wait to hear."

I stomped some of the mud off my shoes and rolled my bicycle on the new grass that was sprouting up around the pond. Eventually, the tires were clean enough that I could ride again. I climbed on and pedaled half-heartedly. My legs were sore. My back hurt, and I was hungry. My best bet would be to call the police station and let them direct Norwich to the killer. I was a hundred percent sure that Remi Seymour had never come up once in his investigation. He was too focused on the easier targets like Jack.

It was those thoughts that had my mind occupied, when out of the blue, Remi jumped out in front of me on the trail. I turned sharply. My cheap little beach cruiser couldn't handle the sudden move. Down I went, bike and all. More pain. More mud. I was done.

"You know, Remi, I've had about enough of—" As I scolded her, the vision in front of me morphed from a tall, long legged woman to a woman holding a big rock. I pushed the bike off of me so fast, the gear wheel gouged right through my jeans and the skin below. I rolled out of the way

215

just in time to avoid the large rock. By the time I sat up and got my feet under me, she'd *reloaded* with the rock. I closed my eyes and held up an arm, ridiculously thinking it might stop the blow from a very big rock.

The next sound was not my own scream of pain but a thump, a growl and a grunt. "I think you've killed enough people this week," the deep, familiar voice said.

I lowered my arm and opened my eyes. Nate had both Remi's hands behind her back. The rock was back where it should be, on the ground. Nate peered around Remi's head. "How you doing, Tiger? Looks like you and your trusty steed got caught in the mud."

I pushed to my feet. Warm blood trickled down the front of my shin. I gave Remi one of my meanest glares.

She looked away. Just months ago, she was a regular woman with a nice job, a sweet little beach cottage and a happy future to look forward to with the man she loved. It was awful to think how love could sometimes transform a person entirely.

"I don't understand," I said, after finally finding my bearings. "How did you know I was up here?"

"Well, I didn't know exactly where I'd find you, and I have to say, the scene I came upon was even more shocking than I expected." He cleared his throat loudly behind Remi as he held her hands behind her back. "But we were on a lunch break at the work site and Rafael's wife called. She told him she'd just seen Anna St. James chasing after Remi Seymour on a bicycle. I figured you might need some help." He glanced down at my frazzled mud covered bike. "We need to get you a better bike."

"I love my bike. Hopefully, I won't have to do a full police pursuit on it again."

"I called the station on my way up the trail to let them know we needed Norwich. He was still on the island. Apparently, he'd been harassing Samuel and Sera. Sam texted me about it. Should we walk down to meet him? Something tells me this hike will be too much for him."

"If you're all right walking her down."

"Not the first time I've had a suspect and no handcuffs available."

Remi didn't say another word the entire walk down, but when Norwich read her her rights she broke down into loud sobs. Jamie watched in shock from afar.

One man with baking skills came to the island. He created more havoc than a hurricane.

thirty-six

IT WAS my favorite time in the evening, dinner dishes cleared away, everyone off to their respective *corners,* and Nate and I had some time alone. The weather was still cool, but the clouds had moved on leaving behind a blue velvet, diamond dotted sky. We zipped up our coats and sat at the top of the back steps with cups of hot cocoa.

"Terry, the sourdough man, got his starter back. Turned out Abner had a spare key to the bakery building. The last owners had given it to him in case of emergency."

"Once again, Anna St. James saved the day. Guess you caught another one," Nate said. "You should've been in law enforcement."

"Ugh. Not for me at all. I much prefer my style of informal investigation. Setting up corkboards, casual chats with people and scooping up the occasional helpful gossip. I could do without bicycle chases."

Nate laughed. "I only wish I'd seen more than just the tail

end of it. I'll bet you were a sight to see pedaling away on that bike, smoke coming off the tires and wind flying through your hair."

"There was no smoke. Only mud. And my hair was drenched from the rain." I wrapped my arm around his. "I'm glad you came to find me. I'm not sure how it would have ended if not for my knight in shining armor."

"Knight in sawdust covered flannel was more like it."

"Who needs armor anyhow? I much prefer flannel." I rested my cheek on his shoulder. "Nate, do you miss it a lot? I saw you today, and I thought, boy, they probably really lost something when Detective Maddon resigned." I don't know why I was picking at this particular topic. Maybe it was better if I knew more what he was feeling. Then I wouldn't be so shocked when he decided to leave.

"Detective Maddon, the man who couldn't catch a killer with a pillowcase. I don't think they're shedding too many tears over it. But I do sometimes miss it." He leaned over and kissed the top of my head. "I'm content right now, Anna. I have more reasons to stay than I do to leave."

I lifted my head off his shoulder and looked at him. "I'm glad, Nate. Cuz I'm getting really used to having you around."

"I'm getting pretty used to being here." He leaned forward, and we kissed on the back porch under the evening sky.

Frostfall Island Cozy Mystery #5

about the author

London Lovett is author of the Port Danby, Starfire, Firefly Junction and Frostfall Island Cozy Mystery series. She loves getting caught up in a good mystery and baking delicious, new treats!

Learn more at:
www.londonlovett.com

Printed in Great Britain
by Amazon

28108147R00130